From Geek
to Goddess

KINGFISHER
An imprint of Kingfisher Publications Plc
New Penderel House, 283-288 High Holborn
London WC1V 7HZ
www.kingfisherpub.com

First published by Kingfisher 2007
2 4 6 8 10 9 7 5 3 1

A CIP catalogue record for this book
is available from the British Library.

ISBN: 978 07534 1165 0

Printed in China
1TR/1206/PROSP/SCHOY/70NEWSPRINT/C

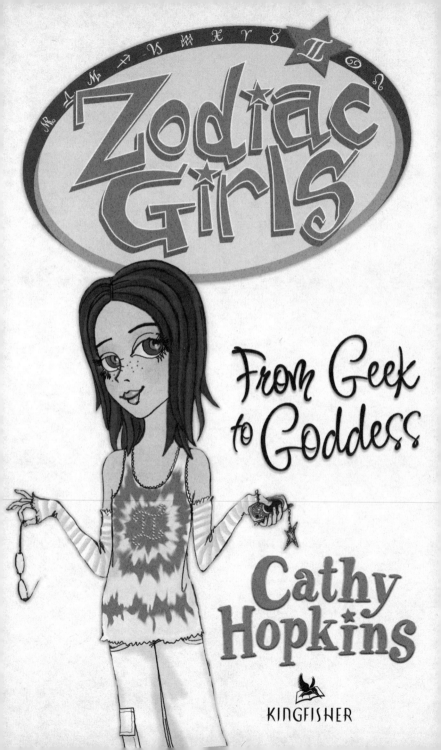

Zodiac Girls

From Geek to Goddess

Cathy Hopkins

KINGFISHER

Chapter One

Blub... blub... blub...

"Goodbye, life," I sighed as I looked down from my bedroom window towards the bus stop at the end of the road.

Everyone was there. All my mates. Lucy. Chloe. Ellie. Jess. Charlotte. They were messing about, laughing and shoving each other as usual. *There's been some almighty humongous mistake. This so isn't right.* I should have been with them. I should have been *going* with them. A new start for all of us, into Year Eight.

I stared down at Jess, willing her to look up. She was my best friend but she'd probably be Charlotte's from now on. I bet she would. She'd soon forget me. It was bound to happen if we went to different schools. She'd said she'd wave to me from the bus stop and she hadn't even looked up. Not once. She'd been too busy having a laugh with Charlotte. Instead of me. *Not going to cry, not going to cry,* I told myself as the bus came rattling down the road and Jess stuck her hand out to wave it down. It was too late, tears stung the back of my eyes and I knew I was going to blub. Again.

I watched my mates get on the bus and disappear off round the corner. And now the road was empty. I was alone.

Well, almost. Bertie, who had been standing, watching with me, paws up on the windowsill, looked up at me sympathetically and let out a soft whine.

I ruffled his black silky head. "And soon I'll have to say goodbye to you too," I sighed as I turned away from the window.

My suitcase was ready on the bed. Mum had packed it for me over the weekend. New clothes. New uniform. Everything I'd need for my new school. I shoved it off the bed and onto the floor, where it landed with a loud thud.

"Well, *that's* what I think of you," I said as I stuck my tongue out at the offending case.

I took a quick glance at myself in the mirror. A ginormous spot stared back.

"Go away," I said to it, but it took no notice and glared back at me defiantly. I'd been lucky so far as I never usually got spots but this one appeared over the weekend to make up for all the months without. Right in the middle of my forehead. If there was a prize for spots, I'd win it hands down. You couldn't miss it, no matter how much concealer I plastered on. And it was one of those that you couldn't pop as it was an under-the-skin, lumpy one that just glistened red and shouted, wa*hey*, LOOK AT ME! Just what you needed on the first day of term when you want to look your best. Not.

"Yuck," I said as I made a face at myself and pulled my hair back into a ponytail. Big mistake. It only showed my Award-Winning Spot off more. *Maybe I should cut a fringe?* I wondered as I pulled my hair loose again. Even my hair was misbehaving today. I so wished I had straight blonde fine hair like Jess's and Lucy's, but no, I had a mass of boring brown kinky hair. I'd tried straightening it with my hair irons but it had still managed to go curly again. *Great impression I'm going to make. I look like a muppet. A spotty muppet.*

"Gemma, Gem*MA*," Mum called up the stairs. "Almost time."

I felt a sinking feeling in the pit of my stomach. This was almost it. Goodbye to my friends. My dog. My cosy bedroom. My life.

I took off my dressing gown and put on the uniform that was hanging ready on the back of the door. Prison outfit more like. Black skirt, cream blouse, yellow and black tie. I had another look in the mirror, hoping that by some miracle in the last five minutes I had turned into Britney Spears and looked

7

like a hot babe, like she did when she dressed in a school uniform for that old video of hers. No such luck.

"Don't call us," I said to my reflection. "We'll call you."

Mum bought the uniform too big so that I could grow into it, only by the look of it, that's not going to happen until around Year Eleven. I looked ridiculous. Anyone could see that the sleeves were too long and the shoulders hung off me. I might be going to a posh school with posh girls, but my parents had to scrimp and save so that I could attend. A new uniform for me every year wasn't an option. *I bet none of the other girls have had to get kit that they can grow into,* I thought. *I bet all their parents are so stinking rich that they can have a new uniform every week if they want. It's so not fair. I don't want to be going to a knobby school with knobby pupils. I want to be going to the local school with my mates, where you don't have to wear a uniform at all.*

The trouble started last summer when some ancient great aunt, (who I'd never met as she lived in America), left some money to my parents in her will. With one condition – that the money was to be used for "a private education" for me. Mum and Dad were over the moon, even though there was one small problem. She hadn't left *quite* enough to cover all the fees. Only two-thirds of what was needed. That didn't put them off. They decided that "fate" had given me a chance and they were going to do all they could to make it happen. Mum got an evening job teaching English as a foreign language on top of her normal job at the library and Dad started putting in extra hours at his garage. All so I could go to private school.

"What a *lucky* girl you are," everyone said.

"Opportunity of a *life*time," I heard over and over again.

No one asked me what I wanted. What I wanted was to kill that aunt. Only she was already dead. No. No one asked me what I wanted at all, and on the rare occasions that I dared to object to being separated from my friends, Mum and Dad laughed and said I'd soon make new ones. They *really* don't understand what changing schools can be like.

I'd tried getting Dad on his own, but he said I had to remember the sacrifices Mum was making for me.

I tried getting Mum alone, but she said I had to remember the sacrifices Dad was making for me.

I tried my grandparents and Grandma said I was in danger of becoming an "ungrateful little madam".

Only Bertie understood.

And so I was off to Avebury, a new school where I knew I wouldn't belong. I hoped that when Mum and Dad saw me cast out as an outsider and failing all my exams they would remember the sacrifices *I* made by giving up my friends and going along with it, just to keep them happy. I had no choice in the end. What with them working all hours and wearing themselves out to give me what they thought was the "opportunity of a lifetime", I couldn't say too much. I didn't want to be seen as an "ungrateful little madam".

By now I was feeling quite sorry for myself so I opened the wardrobe, got in, sat on the floor and closed the door. *Perhaps if I stay here long enough,* I thought, *the back will fall through like it did in those C. S. Lewis storybooks and I'll find myself in a magical land like Narnia.* I knocked on the wood behind the clothes. No such luck. There was no secret door there. Only the back of the wardrobe, then the wall adjacent to the bathroom. I knew it was a silly thought.

Outside there was a scrabbling and a soft growl. I opened the door and Bertie leapt in to sit on my knee. I think he knew something was up. He'd sat in my suitcase last night as Mum packed the last things and he refused to move until she shoved him out. He hated it when the cases came out. He knew from when we'd been on holiday that clothes being packed meant that someone was going away.

This time, it was no holiday.

"It's *so* not fair," I said to Bertie as he licked my face in the dark. "Why did that stupid aunt have to die and leave me money anyway? She'd never even met me. Maybe she was miserable all her life and wanted to make sure that someone carried on suffering after she'd gone. Why couldn't she have left me the money and said, spend it all at Topshop? Now *that* would have been worth having."

"Woof," said Bertie and he began to make himself comfortable in my lap. As he's a border collie, he's not a huge dog, so it wasn't too bad, but I did feel a bit squashed all the same. Not that I minded. His warmth and familiar doggie smell were reassuring.

"Gemma, GEMMA," Mum called again and I heard her footsteps coming up the stairs.

"Shhh," I said to Bertie as we heard my bedroom door open.

"Gemma?" asked Mum's voice.

Unfortunately Bertie woofed in response and a moment later, Mum opened the wardrobe door.

"What on earth are you doing in there?" she asked as I looked up at her from behind the hems of hanging skirts and trousers.

"Nothing," I replied. "Looking for Narnia."

Mum looked at me quizzically. "Narnia? Well, if it was on our list, I'd have packed it. Come on, come out. It's almost time for us to go."

I decided to make one last bid for freedom. I fell on my knees in front of her. "Mum, please, save me from this terrible fate…"

Mum started laughing.

Why does everyone always think it's so hysterical when I'm being deadly serious?

"I know it's a new start," said Mum as she sat on the end of my bed, "but you'll love it when you've settled in."

"Won't," I said as I sat up.

"Course you will. You'll make new friends in no time."

"Won't. Don't want new friends. I want to be with Lucy, Chloe, Ellie, Jess and Charlotte. They're my friends."

"You can still see them when you're home at half-term. Come on, Gemma, this isn't like you. You're a very lucky girl. Avebury is one of the best schools in the country. Loads of girls would love to have your chance."

"Don't care. Don't want to go."

Mum laughed again. "See if you can stick your bottom lip out just a bit more…"

"Hmpf," I replied. "No one *ever* takes me seriously."

Suddenly Mum sighed. "Look, Gemma. I'm not having this conversation again. We've been through it a million times."

"Yeah, but no one asked me what I wanted. I wanted to go with my mates back to the school down the road. That's a good school too. I was happy there."

"We only want what's best for you. This is…"

"I know," I said, "the opportunity of a lifetime. Only my life is over. Please Mum, please. Let me go with my friends. I'll work really hard. We should all be starting Year Eight together today and instead..." I felt tears welling up again, "instead... I'm going to be all on my own. I won't know anyone."

"You'll know Sara Jenkins. She goes there."

I snorted. Mum didn't really know Sara. She lived in a posh house in the next road and thought she was God's gift. Okay, so she had long blonde hair and was really pretty, but she was mean. In the Christmas holidays, Jess and I saw her and her mates at the skating rink outside the town hall. It was our first time and when we fell over, she thought it was hilarious. She pointed at us and laughed. She, of course, had been skating for years and probably had had a private tutor.

"Sara Jenkins will already have a load of mates," I said. "She won't even give me a second glance."

"Well, there'll be plenty of other girls in your position, Gem. You're probably not the only person who will be starting today. Everyone's bound to be nervous, but you'll pal up with people in no time."

"Huh," I said and folded my arms. "People make friends in Year Seven when everyone is starting. By Year Eight, everyone's got their friends. The groups are fixed. The populars. The geeks. The computer whizzes.

The nerds. The sporties. You don't understand how it works."

Mum stood up. "Now don't be childish, Gemma. You're twelve years old and about to start at one of the best secondary schools in the country. You should count your blessings. So enough. It's time for you to start behaving like a young lady. Now finish getting dressed and start acting your age."

I lay on my back. "Huh," I said again. "You really *don't* understand."

"Five minutes," said Mum. "And get up off that floor. Your uniform will be covered in dust."

"Good," I said. "That's how I like it."

Mum rolled her eyes and got a card out of her pocket. "By the way, your dad left this for you before he went to work this morning."

When she'd gone, I ripped open the envelope. Inside was a card with a black-and-white photo of an athlete holding a huge silver cup. Inside, it said, "Winners never quit and quitters never win. So get out there, walk tall and show them what you can do. Love, Dad."

My eyes filled with tears again. I quickly wiped them away. *What is the matter with me this morning?* I asked myself. *I'm turning into a pathetic wet drip and I'm going to have a frog face with bloodshot swollen eyes and a big red nose from snivelling.*

Outside the window, I could see Mum beginning to load up the car. Her normally glossy chestnut (tinted) hair was scraped back into a ponytail and she had the teeniest bit of grey coming through at her temples. *Oh, hell and Horlicks,* I thought. *My fault.* Giving up her regular hairdressing appointments had been one of the sacrifices she'd made to pay for the school. At least Dad didn't have to worry about hair. He'd lost most of it in his thirties. I'd said goodbye to him last night as he started work so early in the morning. He'd looked tired, as he often did on a Sunday evening. I was going to miss him and Mum.

"Ungrateful little madam," I told myself. "Start acting your age. Opportunity of a lifetime. Blah-de-blah-de-blah."

I knew there was no getting out of the situation. I'd tried appealing to their better natures. I'd tried begging. I'd tried rolling on the floor and moaning like a mad girl, and clearly none of it was going to work. I knew how hard Mum and Dad had worked for me, even if I hadn't *asked* them to. Maybe I could go for a term and then they'd realize what a mistake it was and let me come back home. *Yes, there's light at the end of the tunnel,* I decided. *Darkest hour is before dawn and all that.* With those thoughts in mind, I put on my oversized blazer, applied a bit more spot-concealer and brushed my hair.

Bertie was looking up at me with great sad eyes. I felt my own eyes fill up again. *This is ridiculous,* I thought. *All I've done today is blub, blub, blub.*

I bent over and put my hand out to him. He put his paw in it the way I'd taught him when he was a puppy.

"Bye, boy," I said as I shook his paw and stroked his head.

"Woof," he said back.

I straightened myself up. "Right, winners never quit and quitters never win," I said to myself. "It's time to show the world I'm not a quitter. It's walk-tall time. And I'm going to show the world that I can do it."

I took a deep breath, opened the bedroom door, tripped on the carpet and fell flat on my face.

So much for my positive start. I hoped it wasn't an omen.

Chapter Two

Posh school

"Are we almost there?" I asked as we passed through a small village and the road opened up into countryside, with fields and trees on either side.

Mum and Dad had already been out to Avebury to have a look around and meet the headmaster, but so far I'd only seen the brochure and didn't really know what to expect.

Mum nodded. "That's it down there," she said as we saw a huge wrought-iron gate between two brick pillars about a hundred yards down the road on our left.

I could see a grand old house with gables to the left of the gate with an immaculate garden out front. *Chiron House* said a brass plate by the front door. I peered in the windows as we passed and could see a room of old ladies sitting in chairs. Some were staring out of the window, others appeared to be watching television.

"But that looks like an old people's home, Mum,"

I said as panic rose inside me and I wondered what sort of place she was going to leave me in. If that was the staff room, the teachers were way past it.

"It *is* an old people's home," said Mum as she turned left through the gates and past the house. "The school is further along up here. I think in the past, Chiron House might have been a lodge to the main house."

"Maybe it's the sixth-form dorm and they've prematurely aged because of being left without their friends and parents. I think we ought to turn around and go home right now."

Mum laughed. As usual, she didn't realize I was serious.

"Or maybe it's the teachers' quarters," she said as if we were sharing some joke. "It's more likely that the teachers will have prematurely aged, not the pupils. Not surprising, really, it can't be easy."

"You said it!"

"I meant it can't be easy to be a teacher," said Mum as we made our way up the long driveway through eucalyptus trees.

"Oooo, collywobbles," I said as we turned a corner and an enormous old red-brick building surrounded by acres of parkland came into view.

"Exactly," said Mum, looking for somewhere to park amongst the fleets of Range Rovers, Mercedes and BMWs fighting for parking spaces in the courtyard at the front of the main building. "You nervous?"

"Um. Yes. No. Don't know," I replied as I gazed out of the window. I didn't know what I felt. Anticipation. Excitement. Terror.

"It is impressive, isn't it?" said Mum with a quick glance up at the house as she found a space at the end of the drive and began to manoeuvre the car into it. "It looks more like a country hotel than a school."

I nodded. "I wonder if they do breakfast in bed. Make mine a chocolate milkshake and fries."

Mum laughed and switched off the engine. "Ready?" she asked as she smoothed down her skirt.

I nodded again. I wanted to get out of the car as soon as possible because I couldn't help but feel that Mum's little old Ford Fiesta looked well out of place amidst the expensive-looking cars but no one seemed to take much notice. Car doors were opening, shutting, boots slamming, cases being hauled up the driveway by exhausted-looking parents as girls greeted each other with shrieks and hugs. Some older girls slouched inside looking cool and indifferent, like they couldn't wait to get rid of their parents. Others, like me, got out of cars and looked round nervously. I don't think I'd ever felt so small in my whole life. Although I wasn't exactly a junior, as I'd be going into Year Eight, I could see that I was still amidst the little starter squirts, wide-eyed and anxious.

Mum took a letter out of her bag and glanced at it. "Right. We have to look for someone in a yellow T-shirt with Europa written on it," she said, then looked around at the crowd.

"Over there," I said as I spotted a tall girl with long blonde hair by a stone angel near the main door in the courtyard. She had a notepad and seemed to be ticking off pupils before sending them inside. "Yellow's for my house. Europa."

"Okay. You go over and let her know that we're here," said Mum, "and I'll get your bags. You take the little one from the back seat that you can wheel."

I pulled out the wheelie case and made my way over to the girl in yellow and the small group around her. She looked at her pad then up at us.

"Hi," she said. "I'm Fleur Maclean. I'm one of the prefects in Year Eleven and I'll be showing you the ropes. There are four houses in the school, Europa, Io, Ganymede and Callisto. All named after the four moons of Jupiter. Your house will be the same as mine, Europa. First give me your names so I can tick them off. Then go into the main hall, down the corridor on the right and into Room 30 where your house mistress, Mrs Blain, is waiting. She'll direct you to your rooms."

Dutifully we gave our names then trooped into the main hall. I took a quick look at the other girls. There were five of them and they looked younger than me, so were probably new Year-Seven girls. They looked as bewildered as I felt. *At least they're all in this together*, I thought as I looked around for someone else my age who might be starting. *It won't be so bad if there's a few of us and maybe I'll get to share a room with someone really nice. Although it won't be Jess or any of my old mates, at least I might make a friend.*

Mum hoisted my bags after me into the main hall and we looked around. The walls were wood panelled, with corridors leading off in all directions. An enormous staircase led up to a stunning stained glass window of a god-like figure with the sun blazing out behind him. The atmosphere was the complete opposite of my old school, which was a run-down 1950s building that smelt of sour milk and boiled cabbage. Here the air was fragrant with beeswax and flowers, from the many huge arrangements on polished tables around the hall.

"I have to go and meet my house mistress," I said, pointing down one of the corridors. "I'll meet you back here in five minutes."

Mum nodded and, for a moment, looked as young as some of the new inmates.

I was determined to be grown up about things from now on. It was my first day and I didn't want to be put down as a baby from the kick-off. *It is daunting though,* I thought as I hurried to find Room 30. *So many corridors, so many rooms. I'll never find my way around. I must tell Mum I'll need a compass for navigation and a flask and sandwiches for if I get lost.*

I tried one door but it was a broom cupboard. Then another which looked like a cloakroom. Just as I was coming out, Sara Jenkins walked past with her mates, all of whom had the same long blonde highlighted hair.

"Hi, Sara," I said, giving her my best smile.

"Sorry, do I know you?" she asked as she looked me up and down, taking in my uniform (of course, hers fitted perfectly.)

"Um, not really, we live near each other. I'm starting today."

"Bully for you," drawled Sara, then she whispered something to one of her friends.

"Um. Sure you haven't got the wrong uniform on?" asked her friend from behind a curtain of long fair hair.

"Nope, same one as you," I said. "One size fits all. I must be so petite that mine hangs off me whereas yours... well it fits perfectly doesn't it?"

The girl blushed and Sara scowled at me and was about to say something back when a blonde lady with a round face and an enormous bosom came bustling forward.

"New arrival?" she asked, looking at me.

Sara's scowl disappeared to be replaced by a sunny smile. "Yes, Mrs Blain. We were just showing her the way."

"Good girls. In there," she said pointing at a door.

Once inside, she ticked our names off on her checklist, then gave us our room numbers. There were squeals of delight when Sara and her mates realized that they would be rooming together again.

"And you, Gemma…?" she asked looking at me.

"Gemma Whiting, Miss."

"I've put you in with another new girl called Ruth Parker," she said. "You can find your way round together. Room 22 on the first floor of Europa wing. Now if you all go back to the main hall, one of the prefects will show you up and give you your sheet of events for the rest of the day."

Ruth Parker, I thought. *I wonder what she's going to be like.* I was glad I hadn't been put in with one of Sara's crowd, as from the looks they were giving me behind Mrs Blain's back, they had clearly decided I was a bad smell.

Chapter Three
School mouse

"You can go now," I said to Mum after Fleur had shown us up to my room and Mum had unpacked all my stuff.

"No, no, I can stay a bit longer," said Mum as she fussed about, arranging my books on a bookcase to the right of the room.

The room wasn't bad. Quite cheerful, in fact, for a prison cell, with rose chintz bedcovers and curtains and white furniture. It had a pretty view over the gardens and trees at the back.

"Which bed do you want?" asked Mum pointing at the single beds on either side of the room.

"I'll let Ruth choose," I said. I was determined to be friends with my roommate when she arrived. It could be so cool. Being an only child, I'd never had to share my room except on sleepovers. This could be like having a sleepover every night. Maybe Ruth could be the sister I'd never had.

After everything was unpacked, Mum was still

hovering and I was eager to start exploring.

"You can go now, Mum," I said again and pointed to the sheet that Fleur had given me earlier. "I have to be shown round with the Year Sevens."

Mum went pale. "Are… are you sure you'll be okay? You won't be lonely?"

As I ushered her towards the door, I got the feeling she was the one who was going to be feeling lonely.

"I'll be fine," I said as she looked near to tears. "Now you have to be brave, Mum. Come on. Chin up."

She smiled weakly. "It's supposed to be me saying that to you."

I smiled back at her and together we made our way back downstairs and to the car, where she looked like she was going to blub for Britain. I was determined I wasn't going to. I'd done my crying. A part of me couldn't help but be curious and I was dying to look around.

Finally Mum got into the car and drove off and I turned back to face the rest of my first day. Mum needn't have worried about me being lonely. There wasn't time. As the last cars carrying parents disappeared down the driveway, the prefects went into overdrive. We were organised into groups of four and given the grand tour. The school was immense – four wings for each of the houses. There was an Olympic-sized swimming pool and a gym in a modern annex at the back, tennis courts, a vast library and a clinic where we were told that there were doctors, dentists and opticians on call should we ever need any of them. Outside the kitchen of one of the wings, there was a vegetable garden, a hen-house and a small enclosure with a couple of a goats and a donkey. Each house had its own dining room and a common room with a telly and toaster. Finally we were introduced to our matron, who had rooms at the top of our wing with Mrs Blain, though we were told not to go up there "unless there was an emergency".

I was beginning to enjoy myself. It was like I'd been left at a holiday camp and my earlier misgivings were starting to disappear. *It can only get better when I meet Ruth,* I thought. *My very own roommate to share it all with, and like me, she won't know anyone. I can't wait.*

After the tour, the prefects handed out welcome packs with maps, timetables, sheets of information and an invitation to meet at one o'clock in the dining room for pizza and a question-and-answer session. I raced upstairs to the first floor to see if Ruth Parker had arrived yet.

I flung open the door to see a girl lying on the bed reading a book. She was tiny. And I mean tiny – I'm not tall, at five foot two, but she looked like she was only about nine years old. *Maybe she's one of these genius-type people who are way ahead of their age,* I thought.

"Hi," I said. "You must be Ruth. I was wondering where you were."

The girl glanced up nervously and I couldn't help but think she looked like a startled mouse. She even had hair the colour of a mouse, light brown tied back in a severe plait.

"Hello," she said, then went back to her book.

"I'm Gemma. Gemma Whiting. I'm going to be sharing a room with you."

"Oh," said Ruth with another quick glance up. "Okay. I've put my things away. I hope that's all right."

"Course," I said. "It's your room too. Have you had a look around?"

Ruth shook her head. "Not really."

"Well, there are loads of prefects showing people around and pizza in the common room if you're hungry and…"

"No thanks," said Ruth.

"Are you sad to leave home?" I asked.

No answer, just a tiny shrug of one of her tiny shoulders. "My parents have gone abroad, so I don't have a home as such. They've rented it out while they work out their contract in America."

Oh, this is going to be fun, I thought. *Not*. But I couldn't help feeling sorry for her; at least my parents were only a couple of hours away.

"What are you reading?"

"Philip Pullman," she said.

"Is it good?"

Another shrug and a brief nod. *Well, she's lively,* I thought. *But maybe she wants to be left alone. Maybe she's sad about her parents leaving and needs some quiet time.*

I waited for a few moments in the hope that she might say something else, but she seemed deeply engrossed in her book.

"Okay," I said. "I'm going down for some food. I'll be back later."

Another shrug. So I left.

I made my way down the stairs and into the common room, where a crowd of girls were tucking into lunch. I wished Ruth had come down with me so that I had someone to talk to, because apart from the Year Sevens, all the other girls already knew each other.

I went to the buffet table and helped myself to pizza, then looked for somewhere to sit. There was one space on a table where Sara Jenkins and her mates were sitting. Sara saw me eye the spare chair and she quickly put her bag on it. I got the message – not wanted there… I made my way over to the window and pretended to be fascinated by the view. *I hope Ruth livens up a bit,* I thought as I stared intently at a rose bush and tried not to look too self-conscious. *I don't like this awkward feeling of not knowing anyone.*

The common room looked out onto the front and in the distance I could see a motorbike coming up the driveway. Then I heard someone say, "Oh, here's Hermie," and a group of older girls rushed out. I took a closer look to see who was on the bike. Whoever he was, he was tearing down the driveway at full pelt. For want of anything better to do or anyone to talk to, I decided to go out and join the group of girls who were by now waiting in the courtyard.

"Who's Hermie?" I asked a girl with short dark hair who'd obviously had the same idea.

"Don't know," she said as we reached the front, "but his bike looks cool."

As Hermie approached and saw the gathering crowd, he got up on his feet on the seat and did a handstand on his handles. The crowd gasped in admiration. I caught my breath as I thought he was going to fall off any minute – what he was doing looked really precarious. He didn't stay up long, though, and swung back down into the seat, revved up, reared the front wheel up into the air and screeched to a stop outside the main door. There he turned off his bike, took his helmet off, ran his fingers through his glossy shoulder-length dark hair, shook out his hair some more and gave his admirers a huge smile. All the older girls, including Fleur, went red and smiled coyly back at him. He was clearly a hit with the Year Elevens.

I laughed. It was like watching a shampoo commercial where some impossibly handsome model flicks perfect hair this way and that way for the camera. Like – flickety-flick. *Look at me. I'm so gorgeous.* I had to admit that he *was* good looking though, like one of those statues of a Greek god. I was just trying to work out how old he was – maybe nineteen, maybe in his twenties – when an elderly man with white hair and a beard came rushing out of the front door. He looked furious.

"Oops," said a girl behind me. "Here comes trouble."

"Who's that?" I asked.

"Headmaster," said the girl. "Dr Cronus. Stay out of his way if you can. He can be a real taskmaster if you get him in the wrong mood."

"And what sort of insane display do you call that?" yelled Dr Cronus. "This is a school, for heaven's sake, not a circus."

Hermie grinned. "Hi, Grandpa," he said. "Delivery for one of the girls."

Dr Cronus then turned to the crowd of girls. "And what are you lot gawping at?"

I looked at the floor and shuffled about, trying to pretend that I wasn't really there. I didn't want to get in trouble on my first day.

Dr Cronus sighed. "For the sake of the new girls,

I suppose I'd better introduce you," he said to Hermie. "Girls, gather round. This is Hermie. He's our messenger boy. If any of you have post, he'll take it and he will also bring our post and packages from outside to us. All post can be left in the main hall in the box saying post."

One of the girls giggled and Dr Cronus gave her a stern look.

"And what's funny about that?" he asked.

"Er… nothing," said the girl. "Nothing at all."

Hermie took off his leather jacket to reveal a black sleeveless T-shirt with the words Mercury Communications on it and toned, tanned arms. I also noticed that he had a tattoo of a planet on his right arm and four star-shaped earrings in his left ear. He didn't look like the grandson of Dr Cronus at all as the headmaster looked like he belonged to another ancient age. Hermie was well fit, and definitely of this century. He gave a little bow and another of the girls giggled, then quickly stifled it when she saw Dr Cronus look at her.

"Only one package today," said Hermie, producing a parcel from the back of his bike. "Ta-DAH! For the one and only Gemma Whiting."

I felt myself go red as everyone looked round to see who Gemma Whiting was. I put up my hand and made my way forward.

Hermie looked right into my eyes before handing me the parcel. I felt myself go even redder, even though his expression was kind. "Ah. So it's *you!*" he said. "Your lucky day, babe."

I took the parcel from him. "Er… thank you very much."

By now even more girls had come out, including Sara and her mates. Everyone was looking at me and at my parcel.

"Have a good day," said Hermie as he tied his jacket round his waist, jumped back on his bike, put his helmet back on and revved up his engine. He gave his grandfather a cheery wave, then took off. As he passed Sara and her friends, he spun his front wheel so it made gravel from the drive fly up and hit their legs. Sara leapt back and as Hermie rode past me, I swear he winked at me.

"Okay. Enough of this," said Dr Cronus. "Settle down now. Back inside." And he disappeared off through the front door.

"What is it?" asked the dark-haired girl as a crowd now gathered round me. "What have you been sent?"

"Don't know," I said as I tore the package open. All eyes were on me once again and I felt a mixture of curiosity and embarrassment at being the centre of so much attention.

Inside was a turquoise glittery mobile phone

wrapped in bubble wrap, a silver pendant and a card. The phone was state-of-the-art designer fab and the pendant was delicate and exquisite. Both items looked like they had cost mega bucks and I wondered who on earth could have sent me such gorgeous things. *There must be a mistake,* I thought.

"What's on the chain?" asked one of the girls, looking closely at the pendant.

"Looks like a Zodiac symbol," said Fleur. "Yes. It's the twins. For Gemini. Is that your star sign, Gemma?"

I nodded. Maybe it wasn't a mistake.

"Same as me," said Fleur. "I'm Gemini too, so that's how I knew."

"And *cool* phone," said one of her friends.

"What does the card say?" asked Sara who had suddenly decided to take an interest.

"Don't know," I said as I read the card. I was hoping that it would tell me who the gifts were from, but there was no message on it. In fact, it looked like a business card with an address on it on one side, and on the other side, in small print, there were a few facts about Gemini.

Gemini: an air sign, rules the arms, chest and lungs, colours are yellow and silver. Lucky day: Wednesday. Birthstone: crystal/agate/emerald. Keywords: lively, communicative, adaptable, multi-faceted, sharp-witted, mentally active, independent. Ruled by Mercury.

"Don't know much, do you?" scoffed Sara and she reached out and grabbed the phone. "Neat phone, though." She flicked it open. "I think it's one of those video camera phones." She pressed a few buttons but the phone appeared to be dead. I wanted her to give it back to me as it had been sent to me, not her, but she didn't seem in any hurry to hand it over.

One of her friends snatched the card and began to read it out. "It's a website address," she said as she turned it over and read the other side as well. "For some zodiac thing. Huh. Are you a new-age nut then, Gemma, into astrology?"

I took the card back from her. "No," I said. I was as baffled as everyone else was by the mysterious gifts. *Who could possibly have sent them?* I wondered. *No way could my mum or dad or my mates have afforded things like that.*

In the meantime, Sara was roughly pressing all the buttons on the phone, trying to make it work. Suddenly an image appeared on the screen. It looked like a green blobby monster and Sara leapt back, but not before the face in the screen was joined by the words, "Get OFF me, Madam Snotface."

A couple of girls who were close enough to read the message burst out laughing and Sara dropped the phone like it was a hot brick.

"I don't like it," she said. "It's weird." She linked arms with her friends and sneered at me. "And you're weird. You can keep your stupid phone. And your necklace. It's probably a cheap giveaway for some sad promotion, anyway."

It's not a cheap giveaway, I thought as I picked the phone up from the ground to see that a new face had appeared on the screen. It was an image of Hermie smiling and giving me the thumbs-up. *Wow,* I thought. *It's one of those camera phones. I've always wanted one of those, but... where did the green thing disappear to?* Sara was right. The whole thing *was* weird but I wasn't going to give her the satisfaction of seeing that I was fazed by it. I glanced up to see that some of the older girls were looking suspiciously at me.

"So who sent you the phone?" asked Fleur.

"Not sure," I replied as I clicked it shut. "Um. Probably my dad or someone."

"So did Hermie leave you his number?" asked Fleur.

"*Me?* No. No way," I said and glanced down at the card. The girls clearly fancied Hermie and didn't like the thought of any competition. "I think Sara was right. The card is probably some sort of a promotion for an astrology site. Probably put in the bag when whoever bought my pressies got them. You know how it goes. Sales assistants are always putting all sorts of stuff in bags with your purchases to advertise stuff. Pizzas. Free mobiles. Holidays in the Caribbean. Zodiac stuff. Not my thing."

I was aware that I was rambling and ought to shut up. "And… anyway, even if Hermie had left me his number, which he hasn't, I'm not into boys or anything. Yeah. I think I might as well bin the card."

"Round the back, outside the kitchens," drawled one of Fleur's friends as she flicked her hair off her face then slouched back inside.

Phew, I think I handled that okay, I thought as I made my way round the back to get rid of the card. It was going to be hard enough with Sara and her lot treating me like a reject. The last thing I needed was the Year Eleven girls taking against me as well.

Chapter Four
Party time

"Winners never quit and quitters never win," I said to Ruth, who was at her desk with her head stuck in a book, as usual. We'd just had supper and were supposed to be doing homework, but I had other plans. I put my books away and stuck my Dad's card back up on the notice-board above my desk in our room.

It was our third day, and besides Ruth, I still hadn't made any new friends. We were the only new girls in our year and as I'd foreseen, the groups of friends in our class were already well established. It was hard getting in with anyone. Not that anyone – apart from Sara and Co. – was unfriendly, they just didn't need new friends. So it was me and Ruth. Ruth and I. Not that I could call Ruth a friend. She was as silent as a shadow. She never spoke to anyone, only answered if a teacher asked her a question. The holiday-camp atmosphere hadn't lasted long and we'd got stuck into our lessons the day after induction. In all of them,

Ruth acted as though she wanted to be invisible. She attended her classes, did what was asked of her and then got back onto her bed with one of her books as soon as possible. I wanted more. I'd seen the groups of girls in the dining room or in the common room, gossiping, catching up, having a laugh the way I used to with Jess and my mates. I wasn't about to give in. *I've always had friends, I'm a Gemini and Geminis LIKE people, like being with people,* I thought. *I want to be in and out of someone's room, chatting, swapping stories, telling jokes, finding out what's happening. I'm not about to become a loner now.*

"I think we should have a midnight feast," I said, "only not at midnight as that's too late. At ten. A ten o'clock feast. You know that saying – if you want a friend, be a friend? That's what I'm going to be. Everybody's friend. Starting tonight. I've done some invites on my pink notepaper asking everyone to come here and I'm going to go and put them under everyone's door while people are in their rooms doing their homework. It's bound to work. There's not much on telly tonight, so who could resist? I've got crisps and liquorice allsorts, a whole load of goodie supplies that Mum left me for the term."

Ruth looked up and I could see panic in her eyes.

"Is that okay with you?" I asked.

"But… but it's lights out at ten."

I rolled my eyes. "I know. That's the whole point. Having a feast when you're supposed to be tucked up in bed."

"But it's against the rules. We'll... you'll get in trouble."

"No one will know. It'll be fine, but is it okay with you? I mean, this is your room too and... well... you need to make friends too."

Ruth shook her head. "Me? No. I'd rather not. But then I don't want to ruin it for you. I'll... I'll go to the library."

"Oh *please* don't do that, Ruth. Anyway it will be closed. You won't have to do much. I'll do all the talking. I just think I... we... need to put out the hand of friendship. If you disappear, people will think you're stuck up or you don't like anyone or something."

"I'll go and have a bath then. A very long bath," said Ruth then she sighed. "I just want to be left alone."

I sighed. "I'd gathered that."

Ruth sighed again. "Sorry."

I sighed again then I laughed. "Look, we can't spend the whole term with both of us sighing every minute..."

But Ruth wasn't listening anymore. She was gathering her bath stuff together for later.

"Okay," I said. "I won't push you. I want *us* to get

on at least. You have a bath if you want. And take some of my coconut-and-vanilla bubble bath. It smells fab."

Ruth gave me half a smile. "Thanks," she said as I went back to my invites and sprinkled a little glitter in all the envelopes. When they were done, I delivered them to all the rooms on our floor and even to Sara Jenkins and her friends, Mercedes, Tasha and Lois, as I didn't want to leave anyone out. It would be great. Everyone would be able to come, as what else were they going to be doing? They'd be so pleased to have been invited and mine would be the very first party of the term.

When I'd delivered the last invite, I went back to my room and got out all the supplies: pop and crisps and chocolate-chip cookies. At five minutes to ten, Ruth got up to go and have her bath, but before she left, she opened her bedside cabinet and got out a bumper bar of milk chocolate.

"Here. This is for your ten o'clock feast," she said then she scurried out before I could persuade her to stay. I broke the chocolate up into pieces and put it on a plate next to the other goodies. Then I waited.

And waited.

And waited.

I got my new mobile phone out for the tenth time since I'd got it to see if whoever had sent it had left a message or better still, thought to give me some free talk time with which I could call my old mates, but there was nothing. Not the strange face and voice that was rude to Sara. Not the image of Hermie. Neither instructions, nor a message, nor a text. *What's the point of it?* I asked myself as I put it back in the drawer.

Five past ten.

Ten past ten.

Quarter past.

Nobody.

I opened the door to check that the number 22 hadn't fallen off by mistake, but no, it was still there.

Twenty past ten. Still no show. Where was everyone?

I opened the door to see if anyone was coming, but the corridor was empty. I went down to the common room to see if maybe everyone was watching TV but there were only two Year Elevens in there – Fleur and her mate Sophie.

Maybe they're all asleep, I thought, but as I made my way back up to my floor, I could hear the sound of laughter down at the opposite end of the corridor to where my room was. I followed the sounds.

It was coming from Sara and Mercedes' room and inside I could hear Sara's voice and then Lois's. *They must be having their own ten o'clock feast*, I thought. Already they'd established themselves as the cool girls of our year and I hadn't really expected them to come to my room. They would see it as beneath them to hang out with a new girl who hadn't proved herself to be as popular as they were. Sometimes I think there must be an unspoken law that goes: "If thou art one of the prettiest girls in class, thou shalt not hang out with less pretty classmates with whopping great spots on their foreheads." But then I heard what sounded like Imogen's voice, and she's not mates with them. She's in the room next to mine with Rose Watson. I pressed my ear to the door. There was definitely a whole crowd of people in there and it sounded like they were having a really good time.

Suddenly the door opened and Rose came flying out. "Ooomf," she said as she crashed into me. "Oh Gemma. Sorry. Didn't see you there."

Now I could see into the room and everyone from my floor was there. Everyone except Ruth and me.

"Oh," said Mercedes getting up off the bed. "Gemma."

I wanted the ground to open up and swallow me. "Yes. Sorry. Um…"

Tasha got up and stood next to Mercedes. "Hi Gemma. Um, yes. We didn't invite you because… because… "

Mercedes took over. "Because we knew that you were having your own party…"

"That's what gave us the idea, in fact," added Lois with a fake smile.

"Yes…" Tasha stuttered, "and that's why we didn't invite you, because, er…"

I could see she was desperately trying to think up some excuse, but it wasn't coming to her very fast. However, unlike Sara and Mercedes, she looked embarrassed. I thought that she might be nicer than her friends as sometimes I'd caught her looking at me, and once she even smiled.

"We thought you were babysitting your mouse," laughed Sara from the bed where she was curled up like a cat.

Everyone laughed. In one way I couldn't blame them, because I'd thought the same thing on my first day. Ruth did resemble a mouse. A sweet mouse but a mouse all the same.

"Doesn't matter," I said as I began to stumble back down the corridor. "Um. Just thought I heard something. Never mind."

Mercedes shut the door and for a moment there was silence. Then I heard them all burst out laughing at the same time.

I crept back into my room and closed the door. All the laid-out food looked so pathetic and Ruth's chocolate was beginning to melt. I was so hurt, it felt like someone had kicked me in the stomach, so I got on my bed and curled up against the wall. I wished I had Bertie there with me to make me feel better. He'd never reject me or have a doggie feast with his friends without inviting me. Dogs aren't like that. They're loyal. Girls can be so mean. There'd been a gang of them at my last school, but I'd never been on the receiving end of their nastiness. Chloe, Jess, Ellie, Charlotte and I looked out for each other. For the first time, I wondered if there had been girls like Ruth, and now me, at my last school. I'd been so busy having a great time with all my friends, I'd never noticed or thought to look.

I really wanted to talk to Jess but it was almost eleven. Her mum would kill me. And talking to her might only make me feel worse. She'd phoned on Monday night from Ellie's house. All the gang was there and they'd passed the phone around and said how much they were missing me. Didn't sound like it. It sounded like they were having a whale of a time. Last night, I'd phoned them again, one by one, and I'd soon used up half of my phone vouchers as they filled me in on the gossip from my old school. I hadn't said too much as I didn't want to admit that in my first week of school, I was the outsider and I was having a miserable time.

I thought about calling Mum. She'd be home from teaching her classes at the night school, but I decided against it. I didn't want to upset her, and she'd probably think I was a baby for feeling like this in the first week. *Only one thing for it,* I thought, as the plate of chocolate stared up at me with a dark, velvety smile.

I'd eaten half the bar when there was a timid knock on the door. I sat up and smoothed my hair. Maybe someone had realized how cruel they'd been to leave me out, and had come to apologise.

"Come in," I called.

The door opened a fraction and Ruth popped her head round.

"Is it okay to come back in yet?" she asked.

"Oh, yes," I said turning back to the wall.

"Has everyone gone?" she asked as she crept in.

"No one even turned up."

"Oh."

"Yes. Oh."

I heard Ruth pad over to her side of the room and the bed creak as she got onto it. I glanced over my shoulder to see that she had taken up the same position that I'd been in a moment earlier. So there we were, rejects, both lying on our beds with our faces to the wall.

I turned and lay on my back and looked at the ceiling. I felt like I was going to burst. "Ruth, have you always been so quiet?"

"Um. Suppose."

"But why? Don't you ever want to talk to someone? Say how you're feeling? Find out what other people are feeling?"

"No."

More silence as I continued staring at the ceiling. Ruth had started reading. *Ah well, never mind,* I thought as I got my Harry Potter book out of my bedside cabinet. Harry had had a hard time with Draco Malfoy when he first went to his boarding school. Maybe I could find some good advice on how to handle mean girls in the book. *Probably helps if you're a wizard like Harry, though,* I thought as I read a few pages. Now that would have been something, if instead of being given a useless phone, I'd been given a magic wand. I could have turned Sara, Mercedes, Lois and Tasha into toads or monkeys or puddles of green slime or made them sprout hair from their foreheads and grow boils on their bums and make their hair drop out and grow back frizzy and bright orange. For a while, I lay on the bed having a most enjoyable fantasy of what I could do if I had magical powers, but as the minutes ticked on, my imagination began to run dry and I couldn't deny the fact that I wasn't at a school with Harry Potter, a boy who had great adventures. I was at a school with Ruth Parker, a girl who didn't want to leave her room if she could help it. I wasn't a witch. I was me. Plain ordinary me.

Miles from home. On a bed, at a boarding school, with no friends. It stank.

"Ruth?"

"Yes."

"Have you ever had any mates?"

Ruth looked over at me with her great sad eyes and nodded. "One. Naomi. She went to live in Australia."

"And after that?"

"Not really. My family was always moving around so I was always the new girl. I stopped trying after a while."

"But why? Everyone needs friends. It makes life so much better."

Ruth shook her head. "I... I got picked on after Naomi went. It's best just to be quiet. The best way to survive is not to bother anyone. You don't get hurt that way. If you hadn't tried to have that midnight– I mean, ten o'clock feast, you wouldn't have got hurt and now look, you're upset."

It was the most I'd heard her say since she'd arrived. And she was right. So much for my "if you want a friend, be a friend". No one wanted to know me. No one had come to check that I was okay and hadn't been upset. I settled back down to my book. Maybe I'd become a bookworm. Get ahead with all my coursework. And I could always catch up with my mates at half-term. I got up to calculate the days left until half-term. It was a long time. Day after day with no friends. Seven days at half-term with friends. It didn't sound like much fun.

I tried reading again but couldn't concentrate. I didn't want to spend my life without any friends.

"No. I'm *not* giving in," I said to the ceiling. I glanced over at Ruth to see if she was going to comment but she'd put her headphones on and hadn't heard me. *Huh,* I thought, *why did I get landed with you? It's not fair. You don't want any friends but I do. And if I'd got another roommate it might have been okay. It's so, so, so not fair. I'm in danger of becoming like you if I don't watch out, a timid little thing who's scared to try anything, and that's not me. Maybe it's just a bad patch. Darkest hour just before dawn and all that. I wish someone could tell me that it's going to get better.*

"It's your lucky day," that stupid messenger boy had told me on Monday. *Just shows what he knew,* I thought. *So why did he give the phone to me? Maybe there was something I missed. Some button I haven't pressed.* I got off the bed and got the phone out of the drawer. I switched it on and was about to try pressing some buttons when it bleeped that there was a message for me. It was so unexpected that I almost jumped out of my skin. I threw it across the bed in case it did anything strange, and then sat and watched it for a while. It didn't appear to be doing anything too odd, just lying there innocently, so I picked it up and opened the message.

"Go to your computer and visit the site," it said.

I scrolled down for the rest of the message.

There was no rest of the message.

What site? I thought. Then I remembered the card Hermie had left me. It was for an astrological site. Why had I thrown it away? Because I was trying to smarm my way in with the senior girls by showing that I wasn't into boys, that's why. But maybe this Hermet or Hermie or whatever he was called had been trying to tell me something. Maybe the stars were in a bad place for me but the phase would pass.

I quickly grabbed my jacket, let myself out of our room and crept downstairs. Everywhere was quiet and the main lights were switched off. There was just a glow from the night light down in the hall. *I wish I'd brought a torch*, I thought, as I tiptoed along to the dining room, then through into the kitchen and prayed that the back door was open. Boris, the school tabby cat, was asleep on one of the windowsills at the back of the kitchen. He lazily opened one eye then fell asleep again.

"Good cat, good Boris," I said as I tried the door.

It was locked, with two enormous bolts, one at the top and one at the bottom. I pulled back the bottom one then pulled over a chair to reach the top one. Two minutes later I was outside.

The moment I stepped outside a security light came

on and flooded the area. I darted behind a wheelie bin, where I giggled to myself. Not because it was funny but because I was feeling nervous. Although I'd joked about the school being a prison, this was like in the movies when a prisoner tries to escape. *Any minute now,* I thought, *a siren's going to wail and the teachers are going to appear at the windows with guns.* I glanced up but the windows were dark. It was going to be okay.

There were three enormous wheelie bins to the right of the kitchen door. *Now which one did I throw the card into?* I asked myself. *And why am I even doing this? It's mad. Why don't I just text Hermie back and say I lost the card? No, better not,* I decided. He might think I was ignoring him, and after earlier this evening, I knew only too well how horrible that felt.

Okay, winners never quit, I thought as I hoisted myself up onto a pile of boxes and climbed into the first bin. *Thank God those security lights are on,* I thought, *or I wouldn't have been able to see a thing.*

I spent the next five minutes sifting through bin bags full of vegetable peelings, bits of old paper and rotting fruit. It smelt *disgusting.* Of decaying meat and bad eggs mixed with a bit of mouldy custard. Not my favourite pong.

And then I saw it. The card was stuck to the side of the bin at the top on the right. I pulled it off and began to climb out.

Suddenly a window opened on the first floor and a face peered out. It was Sara and she was soon joined by Mercedes.

"Is someone out there?" called Mercedes.

Sara looked over the area as I ducked down, but too late. She'd seen me. I heard her snort back laughter.

"It's Gemma Whiting! There. In the rubbish."

Mercedes looked over to where she'd pointed and burst out laughing too. "Aw, Gemma. Not had enough supper, baby? Feeling a bit hungry-wungry?"

"No. Someone put her out with the rubbish," sniggered Sara.

"Neither, actually," I said as I climbed out as gracefully as I could, which was hard, seeing as I had to hoist my leg up, then haul myself over the side. "Actually, I lost something."

Then I pulled myself up tall and tried my best to look as dignified as possible. A difficult feat with a banana peel on my head and a leaf of cabbage stuck to my left ear.

Chapter Five
Zodiac Girl

Ruth was asleep by the time I got back to our room. I waited until the next morning when she'd gone to the bathroom, then I quickly opened my laptop. I went to Internet Explorer, where I typed in the astrology website address.

Soft space-age music began to play as a night sky full of stars and planets appeared on the screen. As it downloaded, a pale blue form appeared, asking for my name, birthday and place of birth. I dutifully typed them in and pressed the submit button.

A second later, the screen burst into life and if no one was awake on our floor, they would have been then as a fanfare of trumpets blasted out of the computer and the screen lit up with flashing lights and bursts of fireworks.

"Wow!" I said as I leapt back in my chair. "What the…?"

"Congratulations, Gemma Gemini," flashed a message across the sky, "YOU are this month's

ZODIAC GIRL." And the fanfare grew louder, tan-tan-na-da DA DA DA DA DA.

The form on the screen swirled about a bit then disappeared and what looked like some sort of map with lines all over it took its place. *Your personal birth chart*, it said underneath. After that there were pages of writing. Sun in Gemini, Rising sign is Aries, Moon in Cancer, Mars is in Aries, Venus in Cancer, Uranus in Capricorn and on it went saying that this planet was here, that planet was there. None of it made any sense to me, except that I was a Gemini. And I already knew that, as my birthday is on May 26th.

So what? I thought as I scanned the pages. *Why does Hermie want me to know all this, unless he's some kind of astrology enthusiast?* I was just about to shut the computer down when a blurry message flashed onto the right of the screen.

"Hey Gemma. Gemini. Zodiac Girl. Ruled by Mercury. Ask for help. You'll get it."

And that was it.

The screen went back to playing its spacey music again. *So big deal. I'm a Gemini with Aries rising or whatever. Is that it?* I felt disappointed. I don't know what I'd been hoping for, but this certainly wasn't it. There weren't any words of wisdom to see me through and it certainly wasn't going to help me make new friends by advising me what to do or say. Like, "Hi there,

I know you might have thought I was mad at first and a bit spotty at the moment but hey, wait a minute, I'm a Zodiac Girl!" And everyone would fall at my feet. Pfff. The site was a letdown. But it *had* said to ask for help and I'd get it. *Ask who for help?* I wondered.

I went back to the mobile phone to see if maybe I'd missed something and there was a clue as to what I should do next.

There was nothing in the inbox except an image of Hermie looking very pleased with himself. *Ah well,* I thought. *Never mind.* It was still a cool phone, so maybe I'd be able to use it instead of my boring old one. If nothing else, I could use it to call my mates. I pressed the button for the address book and found that someone had already got there before me.

Hermie.

Hermie again, I thought. *What a cheek. Who does he think he is, leaving his number? What a big head. He may have half the Year Elevens swooning over him, but not me. I bet his plan is to give a phone to all the new inmates over the next weeks. He probably got them free with his job at Mercury Communications and giving them away was his way of getting everyone's attention. Well, not me, pal.*

I decided to phone and tell him so.

"Hey, Zodiac Girl," he said when I got through a moment later.

"Yeah. It's me. Gemma Gemini. Who's not going

to be part of your fan club just because you gave me a mobile phone with a photo of you looking particularly smarmy. I'm sorry, but you're not my type. Waaay too old. And I don't go for the motorbike thing." Then I thought I might have hurt his feelings, as I had read in one of Chloe's mags once that it's hard for boys, having to take rejection. "Look, sorry, but I don't fancy you, and anyway, I'm only in Year Eight. No hard feelings."

Hermie seemed to be having a laughter fit at the other end. "Sure, no hard feelings," he chuckled. "But did you look at the site properly?"

"Yeah, it said I get help for a month. And that was it."

"Look again," said Hermie. "Come on, Gemma Gemini. Chill out a bit. Give it a go. You've got nothing to lose. Go back to the site. I think you'll find something you might like there. Your birthchart is well aspected by Venus this week."

"Aspected?"

"It means where your personal planets are in relation to each other."

And then he hung up.

As instructed, I went back to the site. At first nothing happened. Then the spacey music started to play again and blurry words appeared. I strained to read them. Something about Pluto being square to Mercury and

Jupiter making me highly persuasive. Renewed energy and for one month, the chance to make my mark and find my calling then a load of stuff about planets being square and sextile. It made no sense to me until a candy pink voucher lined with silver appeared to the top left of the screen. A line at the bottom of it flashed in enormous writing, "PRINT ME OUT." At least I could see that properly.

I'd just printed it out and was reading it when Ruth came back in.

"Oh NO!" I cried. "I don't believe it!"

"What? What's happened?" she asked.

I threw the voucher on the floor. "That pug-faced nappy-bucket poo-bottom of a messenger boy, Hermie. He only sent me some vouchers for a makeover. A *makeover!* Can you believe it?" I felt mortified. How could I have been so stupid? To think that I'd imagined he fancied me. Of course he didn't. He'd singled me out in a glance as the new girl most in need of a makeover! What a *cheek*!

"So what's wrong with that?" asked Ruth.

"Doh. That's why he thought I needed help. He must have thought I was *so* ugly that I need to see a beauty therapist. He must have seen my spot. And my hair. And my uniform."

Ruth picked up the voucher and smoothed it out. "Vouchers for Pentangle beauty salon... and oh, wow,

Gemma, it says that the budget is unlimited. Whatever it takes, whatever the cost, whatever the recipient wants or needs."

"Pfft," I interrupted. "I bet you one of his girlfriends runs the salon and got him to give out these vouchers to get her business."

"Says here that it's for two," continued Ruth as she read what the voucher said. "For this Saturday. And that you have to get your mum's permission. And look, it says there's a class at the salon on Thursday night on how to find your inner goddess. That's tonight."

"My inner goddess? Yeah, right," I said as I took it from Ruth and pinned it on my noticeboard. "I won't ask Mum's permission. She can use them when she comes out this way to visit. No point in them going to waste, but I'm beyond help in the makeover department. And as for my inner goddess, I think she died."

I looked over at Ruth hopefully, but she didn't realize that this was her cue to say, *Oh, no, Gemma, you look fabulous.* Jess always did if I moaned on about my looks, and I always did if Jess was having a horrible-hair day. It was one of those unspoken rules between friends. Ruth just shrugged and looked straight at my spot.

"I think it may be going down a bit," she said, then

looked at my chin. "But you might be getting another one…"

I turned back to the mirror. She was right. Another lurker was lurking lurkily under the skin. It must have been all the chocolate I ate last night. *Huh, serves you right, you stupid thing,* I thought as I reached for my phone. I was going to tell that Hermie exactly what I thought.

"Well, hi there again, Zodiac Girl," he said when he picked up.

"You can take your stupid voucher and stick it up Uranus."

"Oh, very good," laughed Hermie. "Not heard that one before."

"But a makeover voucher. What a cheek! You must think I'm *so* ugly."

"Hey, no way, Gemma Gemini. I told you, your Venus is in a good place. That means she's shining some light on you this week."

"So what? What's Venus? A planet. What can that do?"

"Yeah, Venus is a planet, planet of beauty and harmony. And it's aspected well in your chart, kiddo. I'm trying to help here, not insult you. And don't take this the wrong way, but you're pretty cute for a Year Eight."

For a moment, I was lost for words. That was the

nicest thing anyone had said to me all week. All month. All year. People used to say it all the time when I was little, and in junior school, and even in Year Seven, I could make myself look halfway decent with a bit of effort. But lately, it all seemed to have gone wrong. It felt like I'd got the wrong head on the wrong body and my hair had taken on a life of its own.

"Oh. Thanks," I stuttered. "Um. Okay. And I'm sorry if I made out that you were only giving out phones to add to your fan club."

"Not me, babe. You're the only one that got one. Only one Zodiac Girl at a time. And I'm not some oik out to pick up girls you know, I'm your guardian for the month."

"My what?"

"Guardian. Every Zodiac Girl gets a guardian according to their sign."

"But why me?"

"You're Gemini. Gemini is ruled by Mercury so that's me."

I remembered his T-shirt. Mercury Communications. "But why? How? I mean, why only one Zodiac Girl and why is it me?"

"Someone always asks that! It's you because the stars say it's you. They've lined up in a special way which, to put it simply, means you've got a tough time coming up and the planets are going to help you through it."

"How?"

"You'll find out. Trust me. Just go with it. And read the site properly next time, huh. You may find it useful."

When he'd hung up, I did go back to the site and there, sure enough, it said that Gemini was ruled by the planet Mercury and as a Zodiac Girl, it entitled me to the aid of my personal guardian. Hermie. I felt mystified. Guardian? Ruling planet? Aspects of Venus? What was it all about? And what did Hermie have to do with any of it? Okay, so he worked for a place called Mercury Communications, but he was just a motorbike messenger boy, wasn't he?

When I got down to breakfast, there seemed to be a buzz of excitement in the dining room.

"What's going on?" I asked Rose Watson, who was helping herself to toast and peanut butter from the buffet table.

She nodded her head towards the hall. "End-of-term show," she said. "There's a notice about it in the main hall. For Year Sevens, Eights and Nines."

"Really?"

Rose nodded again. "Auditions will be on Friday afternoon. Proceeds from the show are to go towards building a new science lab. Apparently, if you don't want to be in the show, you can take part in some kind of social-work outreach programme."

No contest, I thought. I knew which I wanted to take part in. Being in a show is one sure way to get friendly with people.

"What's the show going to be?"

"*Bugsy Malone*," said Rose as she moved off to join her friends, Grace and Imogen.

Bugsy Malone! I thought. *Well cool.* We'd done it at junior school and I'd played Blousey, Bugsy's girlfriend. This was heaven-sent. Maybe this was my Venus or whatever being well aspected, the stars lining up to help me like Hermie had said. If that really was the case, maybe I could even get the part I'd really wanted back in junior school. Tallulah. Jodie Foster had played her in the film version, and it was the best role ever. I'd learnt all her songs off by heart in case the girl playing her part got flu or something on the night of the performance. I used to drive Mum and Dad mad singing all her numbers morning, noon and night and sometimes even in my sleep according to Mum. Tallulah was so cool, like a teen goddess. If I could get her part now, I'd be really popular. Whoever played Tallulah always was. It went hand in hand with the part.

I could hardly eat my breakfast, I felt so excited, and went straight to the noticeboard afterwards to sign up for the auditions. To my dismay, there were already four names down for the part of Tallulah. Lois, Sara, Mercedes and Tasha.

Never mind, I thought, *I can audition for both parts, Tallulah and Blousey.* I glanced down to see if anyone was down for Blousey yet. The same names were there. Lois, Sara, Mercedes and Tasha.

If you can't beat 'em, join 'em, I thought as I got out my pen and added my name to the bottom of the list.

Chapter Six
Inner goddesses

As the day went on, the "how to find your inner goddess" class and makeover began to appeal more and more. Maybe it wasn't such a bad idea. And the message on the site had said I had one month to find my calling. *Surely it meant the part in* Bugsy. *It's fated,* I thought, *written in the stars – and isn't that what astrology is all about?*

At lunchtime, I called Mum.

"Gemma, is everything all right?" she asked. "Where are you? You sound like you're in a bucket."

"I'm at school of course. In the cloakroom."

"So why are you phoning now? Is something wrong?"

"No. It's lunch break. Everything's fine. Just, I've been given some vouchers for a beauty salon called Pentangle in the local village, and it says I have to have your permission to use them."

"What vouchers? What are you talking about?"

"Um. Long story. On Saturdays we're allowed to go

into the local village for a few hours. Our house mistress comes with us and brings us back, so she won't be far away and I've checked out the salon and tonight, there's a workshop on goddesses..."

"Oh, Gemma, I'm not sure."

"I won't be on my own. My roommate will be coming with me. There are two vouchers. So please can I go?"

"Well, I'll check with Mrs Blain, then I'll get back to you. But how's school?"

"Great and I'm up for the part of Tallulah in the school play which is even more of a reason that I need to go to the beauty salon."

"So you're settling in all right?"

"Yep. Fine," I said. I wasn't about to tell her that my first four days had been a disaster, the part of Tallulah wasn't actually mine yet and that I had the school mouse as a roommate. She didn't need details, and in any case, all that was about to change. All I had to do was to persuade Ruth.

I found her later in the afternoon in her usual spot on her bed.

"Me? No," she said and got out her book then put on her headphones.

I went and sat cross-legged on the end of Ruth's bed until she finally had to register that I wasn't going to give up on her. Begrudgingly she took off her headphones.

"What?" she asked.

"Trying to be invisible isn't the answer, Ruth. What we need is to change. We both need a makeover. To make the most of ourselves."

"Ah. The zodiac vouchers."

"Yeah. My mum spoke to Mrs Blain this afternoon and they're both okay with the vouchers if we both go. Apparently Nessa, the lady who owns the salon, is related to Dr Cronus and Hermie, so it's not like we're going to see a stranger. And Mrs Blain wants to go to the workshop tonight as she's into goddesses, so no one can object. Can't you see? This is exactly what we need."

Ruth was staring at me with her usual look of panic. "Who, me? Find my inner goddess?"

"Yeah, come on. It will be fun."

Ruth looked doubtful and began shaking her head.

"Oh, come on. *Please*. For me. I want to audition for the part of Tallulah, and she's a real goddess if ever there was one. I'm sure this is all meant to be." I got off the bed and went into one of Tallulah's song and dance routines. When I'd finished, she actually clapped!

"Hey Gemma, you're really good," she said.

"Thanks. I've rehearsed enough times, that's for

sure, and if I can find my inner goddess, I'm sure I'll make more of an impact and I might get a part in the show. And you can find your inner goddess and be more confident."

"But I don't want to be a goddess or in the show."

I sighed. "You don't have to be in the show. I just thought... well, it would be nice to have someone to go to the workshop and the makeover with. Company. And you might get something out of it. And... and if you don't come with me, I can't go. Mrs Blain said I could only go if you came and... no one else is going to come. They all have friends."

Ruth shook her head and put her headphones back on. "Sorry," she mouthed.

I got up off the bed and went to lie on my own. *Life sucks,* I thought as I turned to the wall. *It gives you a break. Then it takes it away.*

I felt close to blub mode. For a moment I'd had hope and now it seemed there was none. I didn't know what else to do.

After a few minutes, I felt a hand on my shoulder.

"Okay," said Ruth as I looked round. "If it really means that much to you, I'll come with you. Not for a makeover or to be a goddess, but to keep you company. That's all."

"You're a top babe," I said and leant over and gave her a hug. She looked nice when she smiled.

"Okay, my lovely goddesses, gather round," said Nessa, the lady running the class.

Goddesses. I had to laugh. It was Thursday night, and as promised, Mrs Blain had given us a lift to Pentangle. I'd been looking forward to it all day. I imagined that the class would be like a session at a model agency with tips on how to walk, how to get made up, hair advice, everything I'd need to land the part of Tallulah.

The décor in the salon was fabulous. It looked like a cross between Santa's grotto and a planetarium with planet mobiles spinning from the ceiling and star fairy lights twinkling around the doors, arches and mirrors. The assembled "goddesses", however, couldn't have looked less divine as we assembled in the manicure room at the back of the salon. The group was:

Mrs Blain and her enormous bosom.

Ruth and her look of panic.

Me and my spots.

A stooped old lady who resembled a tortoise and had brought her knitting along.

A tiny red-haired girl who looked like she was going to burst into tears at any moment.

A tall girl with lank dark hair who was so pale, she looked like a ghost.

On the other hand, Nessa was pure goddess.

Straight out of the pages of *Hello* magazine, she was glamorous and a half, in a footballer's-wife type of way. She was tanned, tall and curvy, with long, highlighted blonde hair, silver stars on her ears and glittery nail extensions. She was dressed in figure-hugging white. A top babe, as Jess's brother used to say.

"Alwight, girls," she said in a strong Essex accent as we gathered awkwardly around her. "As you know this class is to find yer inner goddess. Alwight?"

"Alwight," we nodded back.

I couldn't wait for it to begin. Nessa was so stunning to look at, I felt like a frump besides her. *But not for long*, I thought. If finding her inner goddess had helped her look the way she does, I'd come to the right place.

"Now I want you to have a quick glance at yer goddesses," she instructed, "then we'll 'ave the slide show."

I sat down and glanced at the paper, expecting to see all the contemporary goddesses listed: Madonna, Britney Spears, Kylie, Julia Roberts, all the stars that we see in films and in mags. But no. It looked like a history-homework handout. Pages and pages of it: African goddesses, Asian, Himalayan, Greek, Roman, South American, North American, Egyptian, Hindu…

"Fascinating, isn't it?" said Mrs Blain as she sat next me to and began to read. "I find these ancient entities so interesting."

"Er, yes…" I said as I glanced at my own sheet. The writing was a bit blurry, so it was hard to read, but I could just about make out some of the names:

Branwen. Lady of Love.

Cerridwen. Lady of Inspiration.

Hine-Moa. Passionate Princess.

Kura. Falling Flower.

Inanna. Queen of Heaven.

Allwise. Swan Maiden.

Some of the names sounded lovely and I wondered which one was going to be my inner goddess as I scanned the sheet. I hoped that the slide show would be more informative though. I wasn't really interested in lists of names from history. I was interested in the present.

A few minutes later, the lights went down and the slide show began. *This will be it*, I thought, *she's probably going to show us how to glide on a catwalk. How to stand and move like a goddess.*

But no.

It was a slide show of a load of old statues and sacred sites.

"The power of these names," said Nessa, "and the power of the entities who once claimed these names has been forgotten, the devotion of the faithful considered odd, superstitious even…"

Strange, I thought as I listened. Nessa's voice lost its

Essex accent as she spoke and she sounded more serene and authoritative. *All the same, I didn't come here for this.* Luckily, Mrs Blain got out a box of Maltesers and passed them round, which provided a bit of a distraction. She was riveted by the talk, and even Ruth looked interested. I felt like nodding off. *Where's the make-up lesson?* I asked myself. *The top tips? Maybe this is just the beginning. We'll probably get going on the good stuff later.*

But no.

Nessa told us about the traditions, myths and legends of goddesses in different countries throughout time. Not a word on how to apply your lip gloss. *Peculiar,* I thought as I watched Nessa enthusing on about temples and sacred sites. She didn't look the type to be into that sort of stuff, but she was clearly passionate about it.

After the slide show was over, Nessa asked us all to gather in a circle around a table with an open box on it.

"And now we're going to find our inner goddess," she announced.

At last, I thought.

"I've put the names of all the goddesses on a piece of paper in the box," she said. "Now I want you all to close your eyes and ask your inner goddess to direct your hand to the paper with the name of your personal goddess. I'll go first."

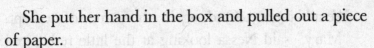

She put her hand in the box and pulled out a piece of paper.

"Graeco-Roman goddess," she smiled then smoothed her hands over her curves and winked. "Venus. Mistress of love, beauty and pleasure!"

"Quite right," said Mrs Blain as Nessa turned to the old tortoise lady.

"Okay," she said. "Your go, Betty."

Betty closed her eyes and put her hand in the box.

"Wotsit say, darlin'?" asked Nessa, her accent back, thick and strong. "Read it out."

"I've got a Central American one," said Betty. "Ix Chel, the lady weaver."

"And that's just what you are, with your knitting," said Nessa with a nod. "Lydia, you're next."

The tall pale girl closed her eyes and picked.

"Northern European goddess," she whispered. "Holda, host of the dead."

Dead right, I thought. *She looks like someone only dug her up this morning.*

"Brill," said Nessa. "Don't look so glum, Lydia. Death often means rebirth in ancient myths. A new beginning." She indicated the box again. "Mrs Blain?"

Mrs Blain closed her eyes and picked.

"Like Betty," she said. "I've got a Central American one too, Mayahuel," then she chuckled and adjusted her bosom. "The many-breasted one!"

We all laughed. Once again, the name seemed apt.

"Mary," said Nessa looking at the little red-haired girl who looked like she'd been crying all day.

Mary took her turn and picked a paper.

"Eastern European goddess. Bozaloshtsh. Lady who cries."

Wow! These are so accurate, it's scary, I thought. *I wonder which one I'll be.*

Nessa turned to Ruth. "What about you, Ruth? You going to give it a go?"

Ruth shook her head and looked at the floor.

Nessa smiled at her. "Come on, love. No one's going to pick on you. You're safe here. You're amongst goddesses."

Ruth hesitated, then got up and picked from the box.

"It's an Egyptian one," she smiled up at Nessa. "Seshat, mistress of books."

Well, that definitely fits! I thought. *She's never got her nose out of one.*

"And last but not least," said Nessa, "Gemma."

I closed my eyes and put my hand into the box. What would it be? Mistress of flowers? Lady of Spring? Swan Maiden?

"Wotsit say, love?" asked Nessa as I read.

"South American goddess, Caipora," I said. I quickly folded up the paper and put it back on the table.

"And what's she the goddess of?" asked Mrs Blain.

"Oh, nothing," I said.

"Can't be," insisted Mrs Blain. "They're all the goddess of something." She put her hand in the box and retrieved my paper, then burst out laughing. "Caipora. The Lady of the Beasts."

I felt myself go bright red as everyone laughed with her. *Typical,* I thought. *There were some beautiful-sounding ones. Ladies of the moon, the forest, rivers or the stars or the sea but no, my inner goddess is the Lady of the blooming Beasts.*

I wished I hadn't come.

Chapter Seven
Showtime

Lunchtime. Friday.

Dear Diary,

Caipora, Lady of the Beasts here. Gemini Zodiac mad girl. That's me.

Life stinks. I'm spotty and ugly and everyone hates me. This week has been the worst ever since time began.

First I meet some weird motorbike messenger called Hermie and he tells me that I'm a Zodiac Girl. He must be having such a laugh with his cousin Nessa or whatever relative she is. Maybe she's his girlfriend and they're in it together. I'm never listening to him again and have thrown his stupid mobile phone in the bins out the back. It didn't work anyway, except to phone him or the beauty salon. I tried putting all my mates in the address book but when I went to call them, the line was dead. What sort of rubbish phone is that where you can only call two people?

And the stupid site he sent me to. Said I have a chance for one month because of some planetary alignments or something and could make my mark. My mark as what? Class geek?

And things are getting worse. Now I have three spots. One on my forehead, one on my chin and one on the side of my nose.

And my hair has got a life of its own.

And even worse than *that*, I was in English today and Mrs Johnson asked me to read out loud and when I couldn't because the page was blurry, she said I needed glasses and I had to go and get my eyes checked by Matron in her clinic and *she* said I needed glasses too. So that's it. I'll be spotty, with glasses. And mad hair. There is no hope for me.

I've tried to get Ruth talking but all she does is read and is the most boring roommate in the history of time. She loved the goddess class and has since got loads of books out of the library about them which have given her more excuses to have her nose permanently in a book. Which is fitting because she is the Lady of Books. Whereas I am the Lady of Beasts. Clearly because that is what I look like. A beast. With glasses. And spots.

I WANT friends. I want to be beautiful. And cool. And be Tallulah in the school show. And I want to be a Lady of Flowers. Not Beasts.

So there. The end. Amen. Ya boo everything sucks. I miss Lucy and Chloe and Jess and Charlotte and Ellie and have now used up a whole month's phone cards talking to them. And they all sound so happy and busy like they have a life. I knew this would happen. I'm all alone in the world. With no one but my spots to keep me company. I wish, I wish, I wish I could play Tallulah. Auditions are this afternoon.

"Hey, Gemma," said Ruth looking up from her book.
"What?"
"What you doing?"
"Writing my diary. Why?"
"Says here in my book that Caipora is a nice goddess. She's the protector of animals."
"So?"
"So I don't think that you should mind that she's your inner goddess. I think you should be flattered. And I've seen that picture by your bed of your dog. Maybe you being the Lady of Beasts means that you're a kind person who likes animals."

You're a kind person, I thought. *Trying to make me feel better but it isn't working.* I knew that I was the Lady of the Beasts because I looked like a beast.

"Have you checked your website today?" asked Ruth. "There might be another message on it."

"No way. I think that Hermie was having a laugh at my expense."

"I thought the class was really good. And I liked Nessa. I don't think she was laughing at you. Or any of us. Take a look."

"Well, I was just going to check my emails, so I guess I could have a peek before the auditions start," I said as I switched my laptop on. "Are you going to try for a part?"

Ruth shook her head. "I'm going to the Outreach programme. Apparently there are hardly any volunteers as everyone wants to be in the show. Sure you won't come?"

"Nah," I said. "Not my thing. What do you have to do?"

"Not much. Visit the old people's home at the bottom of the drive and sit and read to them."

Well that will suit Ruth and her books, I thought, *but I can't think of anything more boring.* I looked to see if there were any emails from Jess or the girls, but there was nothing. *Might have known. They're starting to forget me already.*

I was just about to close down when a pop-up message flashed on from the astrology website.

"Not talking to you," I said as I stuck my tongue out at the screen and stood up from my desk.

Ruth got up from her bed and slid into my place.

"It says 'Lady of Beasts,'" she read, "'protector of animals. Make your mark and find your calling, you have just over three weeks left.'"

"You're making it up," I said.

Ruth looked indignant. "Am not!"

I leant over her and sure enough there were the words she had read out. *This is getting freaky*, I thought as I quickly turned the laptop off. *What is going on? Now even my computer is making fun of me. Either that or Nessa told Hermie about the class and me being Lady of Beasts and they both had a jolly good giggle.*

I was late for the auditions as Matron had been in touch with my mum and arranged for me to see the school's optician early afternoon. He confirmed that I needed glasses, and after testing my eyes, he let me pick a set of frames. Then he said he'd make up a pair to my prescription and have them sent to the school. In the meantime, he gave me a temporary pair.

"You have got to be joking," I said when I looked at myself in the mirror. They looked like the bottom of milk bottles with enormous frames. "These are mad. I look like a clown."

"It's only temporary," he said. "You make sure you wear them, young lady, or you'll be straining your eyes and damaging your eyesight. I don't want to hear that you've had them off, except at night when you're asleep."

Yeah, yeah, I thought. *I've managed so far. I'll stick them in my bag as soon as I get out of here and wait until the half-decent ones arrive, because no way am I going to be seen dead or alive in these.*

"Don't worry," said Matron. "I'll make sure everyone on staff knows that she has to have them on."

Is everyone at this school in league against me? I asked myself as I stumbled out of the room and headed for the drama department. *Don't they know my destiny awaits and I have to get a part in a show?*

The auditions were already well under way by the time I got there and the girls were in the middle of a dance routine. Mrs Woods, the drama teacher, looked up and waved me towards her.

"Auditions for the part of Fat Sam are later," she said as she pointed me towards the benches at the back of the hall where a group of girls were waiting for their auditions.

I was aghast. "Fat *Sam?* No. I'm up for the part of Tallulah," I said. "I know all her songs off by heart."

"Tallulah? But we need a tall blonde for Tallulah and anyway, we auditioned for that part earlier. We're on to Blousey's part now."

Behind her, I could see Sara Jenkins and her mates

wafting about on their toes. I also noticed that Sara had been dancing nearby when Mrs Woods had suggested I play Fat Sam, and had laughed, then passed it on to Mercedes.

"… yes," Mrs Woods continued, "We'd have to pad you out a bit but those glasses are a great idea. Inspired. I think you'd make a great Fat Sam in them. Where did you get them from? The props department?"

"No," I wailed. "The optician said I have to wear them but not for long. With a blonde wig, I could do Tallulah. Oh please. Let me try."

"We haven't got time to go through it all again," said Mrs Woods who was beginning to look harassed. "We've got a whole host of parts to cast."

"Then can I try for Blousey? I did put my name down. Please. Please."

Mrs Woods sighed. "Very well, Gemma, but we've already been through the dance routine once, so just join in where you can. I'll soon see if it's right for you."

I quickly went to the back of the group and watched what they were doing. It was a different routine to the one we'd done when we did the show in junior school but I studied it for a few minutes then began to copy what the others were doing.

Easier said than done. They went one way, I went the other. They'd had time to practise, I was thrown in at the deep end. Mercedes did a balletic leap backwards as I pirouetted forward and I ended up splayed on the floor with my milk-bottle glasses skew-whiff on my nose.

"Oops," laughed Sara.

Mrs Woods clapped her hands for attention and motioned for me to get up. "Right, girls, you can stop there. I think I've seen enough and we've got to move along. I'll post my decision for Blousey later. Now then, those girls at the back who've been waiting, let's see who's right for the part of Leroy next. Okay, everyone who's auditioning, get up and come forward, the others take your places at the back."

I went to sit on the benches at the back and watched as six girls went through Leroy's routine.

"Love your glasses," said Sara with a snide look. "Going for the fishbowl look, are you?" Then she did what I can only assume was an imitation of a goldfish, opening and closing her mouth.

I didn't even bother to reply.

"Oh, you poor thing," said Mercedes. "It must be *so* hard, having to wear glasses."

I didn't reply to her, either. I knew she was being sarcastic. A few minutes later, I heard her sing, "there once was an ugly duckling…" then laugh.

I felt like crying, but I bit my bottom lip and swallowed back my tears. I wasn't going to give them the pleasure of seeing how much they upset me. Not if I could help it.

Later in the day, it was announced that Bugsy was to be played by Mercedes, Tallulah by Sara, and Blousey by Lois.

I was offered a tiny part as an undertaker.

Over my dead body, I thought. *Social services and the Outreach programme, you just got yourself another volunteer.*

Chapter Eight
Makeover madness

At last it was Saturday. Rest and recreation and my first week in the school from hell was over. Sadly, Mum and Dad weren't allowed to visit, because the school said that new pupils needed the first two weeks on their own to find their feet, but all visitors would be welcome the following Sunday. I didn't need to find my feet. I knew exactly where they were – on the end of my legs and ready to start walking out of there. I couldn't wait for Mum and Dad to come so I could tell them how lonely it had been. Hopefully, they'd see sense and get me out and back to sanity. I couldn't wait.

For once, Ruth had her head out of a book and seemed to be getting ready to go out.

"Where are you going?" I asked.

"Oh. Salon," she replied. "Remember the vouchers? Nessa booked us in this afternoon. She told us when we were leaving the goddess class."

I vaguely remembered Nessa saying something, but

hadn't paid too much attention. I was too upset with my inner beastie goddess person.

"Er... is that still all right with you?" continued Ruth. "You did say I could use one of them. Er. Sorry."

"Ruth, you don't have to act like a scared mouse around me," I said. "Sure. Take the voucher. Take both of them. I won't be using them." *It will probably be another lecture on the ancient goddesses through time*, I thought, and I'd learnt enough about them to last a lifetime.

Ruth sat on the end of my bed. "Are you upset about yesterday?"

I shook my head. "Nah," I lied. "Win some, lose some."

"I think you'd have made a great Tallulah," said Ruth. "They don't know what they're missing."

Jess would have said exactly the same if she was here, I thought.

"Thanks." I said.

"I mean it, you'd have been great. So what are you going to do today?"

"Oh, stay here. Read. With these monstrosities of glasses, at least I can see now." Not that the idea of an afternoon on my own appealed that much; I just didn't want to be seen at the moment. I'd had about as much as I could take of being called speccy-four-eyes or the ugly duckling by Sara and her sarcastic friends.

"Oh, please come with me," said Ruth. "It would be

company, and anyway, you can't hide away from the world up here. It's not the answer."

I had to smile when she said that. In one week, we'd done a complete turnaround. Now *she* was the one urging *me* to get out, while all I wanted to do was hide from the world under my duvet.

Ruth got up from the bed and went to my laptop. "Let's see what the site says."

"You can," I said. "I'm really not interested. I mean, so much for being a Zodiac Girl. I thought it might have been a good thing but now I think it's some kind of curse. Like, where's it got me? Nowhere."

Ruth pressed a few buttons on the keyboard. "There's a message for you. From Hermie. He says he's been trying to phone you and that you're not to give up. To trust him. And not to be over-sensitive. He says Saturn will intervene to teach a lesson but Venus is still well aspected for a few more days so make the most of it. Oh come on, Gemma, come with me for the makeover. Please. It would be good to get away from school for a few hours."

"Pffft," I said, as I looked out of the window. "Stupid site. Saturn. Venus. Aspects. What's all that supposed to mean, anyway?"

However, it was a bright autumn day. It would be a shame to stay indoors. Everyone would be going down to the village on the school bus and Ruth would be on her own amongst them. I ought to go, if only to protect her. She looked a right mess. Her hair was back in its usual plait. She was out of uniform and dressed in a grey sack-like pinafore. She looked like she belonged to a past era more than ever.

"Okay, I'll come with you," I agreed. "Give me two minutes to put my jeans on."

Dr Cronus was ticking names off outside the main door in the courtyard where the bus was waiting to take everyone into the village.

"Jenkins, Peters, McMasters," he said with a nod as each girl passed him. "Whiting, Parker."

"Ah, there you are, fellow goddesses," Mrs Blain called down from the front seat when she spotted Ruth and me. "Off for your makeover?"

I prayed that she'd keep her voice down as Sara and her mates were at the back of the bus. The last thing I needed to get out was that I had an inner goddess, that I was Gemma, the Lady of Beasts. They'd love it and I'd never hear the end of it.

Dr Cronus glanced up at Mrs Blain then rolled his eyes to the sky. "Goddesses? Makeover? Frippery! You girls should be going to the library or to a bookshop. Doing something educational to enrich the mind and the soul, not wasting time on superficialities."

He can talk, I thought, as I looked at his tie. If that

wasn't frippery, I didn't know what was. The pattern of stars and planets against a bright blue background was a strange choice for someone who dressed so soberly most of the time. *I bet Hermie bought it for him,* I thought, as the star pattern was like the one Hermie had tattooed on his arm.

Mrs Blain smiled back at him. "Not true," she said. "Life should be about balance, and the girls need some light relief. They work hard enough in the week and deserve a little downtime. And it's not all frippery. We've been discovering our inner goddesses, haven't we, girls?"

"Has that Nessa been doing her goddess classes again?" frowned Dr Cronus. Then he looked directly at me. "There's only one lesson you need to learn, young lady, and that's to love yourself and be yourself."

Yeah, right, I thought as I took a seat behind Mrs Blain. Just shows what that old codger knows about anything. Love myself? I *hate* myself. And be myself? I'd rather be anybody but me.

Ruth sat besides me and nudged me. "Er… did you know that another name for Saturn is Cronus? I read that in my book about gods and goddesses."

"So?"

"Dr Cronus. Don't you get it? The website said that Saturn would intervene to teach you a lesson."

"So?"

"So, Saturn, Cronus."

"She's quite right," said Mrs Blain turning round. "Gods and goddesses often have two names. Like Mercury. In some cultures, Mercury is known as Hermes."

Ruth nudged me again. "Hermes, Hermie."

"Yeah, yeah. And John is also known as Joe and Katherine as Kate," I said. "They're only names."

Ruth shrugged but as we rode on, I began to wonder. Could it be possible that the planets were walking round in physical form? *Nah. Never in a million years. Mad. I'm losing the plot*, I told myself as the welcome sight of shops and the village came into view.

Nessa looked up from doing an old lady's hair and beamed when Mrs Blain dropped us off at the salon.

"I wasn't sure you were coming," she said as she put the finishing touches to her customer. "Hermie said he hadn't been able to reach you on your phone. But I'm so glad you both made it. Be with you in two ticks, just got to finish off here."

While Nessa showed the lady the back of her hair in a mirror, the receptionist introduced Ruth to a beautician called Tracey who marched her off to a room at the back. While I was waiting, I sat down and flicked through a magazine.

"Cup of tea while you wait for your driver?" Nessa

asked the lady who smiled and nodded.

As Nessa disappeared into the back, the salon door chinked open. My heart sank when I saw Sara come in with Mercedes. I quickly ducked down to the side of the reception area, where I could see them but they couldn't see me. I needn't have worried. They weren't staying. Sara glanced round, took one look at the old lady in the chair then declared loudly. "Let's get out of here quick, hairdos for the living dead."

Mercedes giggled and out they flounced.

"You can come out now," called the old lady as soon as the door shut behind them.

I peeked my head up. "Oh, yes… right. Sorry. Just someone I didn't want to see."

"I can understand why," said the lady. "What *rude* girls."

"I know. Sorry about them," I said. "We're not all like that at our school."

"You're from Avebury, are you?"

I nodded and went to stand behind her. Although she looked like she was well into her eighties, her cornflower-blue eyes twinkled with life and she was very elegant in a dove-grey suit, pearls round her neck and her silver hair swept up at the back. I hoped I looked as good as she did when I was her age.

"And… your hair looks lovely," I said. "You mustn't take any notice of them or listen to what they said.

They can be really mean."

"Oh, don't you worry, dear," the lady said then chuckled. "The living dead! Well there's plenty of life left in this old girl, I can assure you. Just you wait and see."

"Here's your tea," said Nessa, who reappeared from the back carrying a tray with a china cup on it. "Now, is it okay if I leave you alone and get on with Gemma?"

"Of course. I'll be fine," said the old lady. "And thank you for the tea."

Nessa took me into a small treatment room next door to the one Ruth was in and once we were alone, she looked me up and down like I was a prize piece of meat.

"Hmm. Best get started," she said. "I like a challenge."

Cheek, I thought but I knew what she meant. My hair was madder than ever and with my glasses, no one was going to look at me twice, except with pity.

She sent me off to a changing room at the back of the salon to put on a robe, and as I was changing, I heard the front door chink open. *Probably the old lady's driver come to collect her,* I thought.

After that, I was pummelled and plucked and waxed and exfoliated and moisturised. At one point, I peeked in the mirror to see what Nessa was doing, only to see that she had covered my face with some pale green gloop. I looked like a ghoul.

Nessa caught me looking and quickly covered the mirror with a huge white towel. "No peeking until I've finished," she said as she produced a pot of cream. "Now. This is my mystery potion for spots. It's full of herbs from the Himalayas in India. They'll be gone in no time. Give me those glasses and I'm going to pop out for a while to see what I can do. You stay here and let the facemask work its magic. Back in a jiffy."

I lay back on the reclining chair and prayed that she wasn't having a laugh at me and that I wasn't going to end up looking worse than I had before. *Nothing to lose*, I thought. *I might as well enjoy it.*

When Nessa came back, she painted the nails on my hands and toes a fab glittery turquoise, then set about cutting my hair.

"Only one thing to do with hair like yours," she said. "We'll keep it long and put some layers in it. It will take the weight out of it."

"Whatever," I said. I was beginning to enjoy the experience. All the lotions and potions smelt wonderful, of roses and jasmine, and I was starting to feel relaxed and light-headed.

After the cut, she blow-dried my hair. "I'm going to pull it straight to give it a shine," she said, "and I've got some great products for taking the kinks out, if you like. You can take them back to the school with you to use there."

"Whatever," I said again, but I was definitely feeling better. To have straight hair was my dream.

For the final touch, Nessa applied a little make-up.

"*Au naturel* for someone your age," she said, "but a little concealer for those spots, a touch of highlighter here and a bit of blusher there won't hurt, and it will bring out your colouring. You're a very lucky girl to have such gorgeous brown eyes."

Hah! I thought, *'gorgeous' and 'me'. Not two words that go together in my book.*

After a couple of hours, she had finished.

"Want to look?" she asked.

"Sure," I said. She couldn't have made me look worse. Nothing could.

She led me to the mirror that she had covered with the towel, then swished it away.

"Ta-dah," she said as I gazed at my reflection. "What do you think?"

I stared at the girl in the mirror. She looked *great*. I couldn't believe it.

"Is that me?" I asked.

"It certainly is," she said. "Every girl has it in her to be a frump or a goddess, and you, my dear Gemma, are definitely of the goddess variety."

"Wow," I said as I gazed at my reflection. "The

Lady of the Beasts has been tamed."

"Indeed," beamed Nessa.

I really did look amazing. My hair was perfect, silky and soft to my shoulders and Nessa had even put some chestnut highlights in.

I turned and gave Nessa a hug. "Thank you *so* much. I don't know how you did it."

"Cheers, darlin'," she said with a smile. "But I only brought out what I saw."

Then I remembered my glasses. "Oh, but I still have to wear the milk bottles. They're going to ruin all your hard work."

Nessa tapped the side of her nose. "When I do a makeover, I do a makeover, and nothing is going to ruin it. I've been over to see the optician and he was just working on your prescription. I persuaded him to get a move on, so here they are. Try them."

I tried the glasses and as everything came into sharper focus, I looked back into the mirror. The glasses were perfect. They were an oval shape with no frame. Best of all, they had a slight rose tint so they looked more like really cool sunglasses than glasses. *No one would call me speccy-four-eyes in these*.

"And I've asked him to make you some contact lenses as well, so you have the choice," said Nessa. "Some days, you won't have to wear glasses at all."

"Nessa, you're a star," I said. For some reason,

Nessa seemed to find this very funny and cracked up laughing.

"Private joke," she said. "That's a good one. Now let's see how Ruth's getting on with Tracey next door."

We knocked on the door. "Just a mo," said Tracey and opened the door.

"Omigod!" I said when I saw Ruth.

"Omigod!" said Ruth when she saw me.

She looked fab. Tracey had got rid of Ruth's plait and cut her hair into shoulder-length layers. She'd even put in delicate blonde highlights. Ruth no longer looked like a scared mouse. She looked very pretty. Delicate but pretty.

"Ruth, you look amazing."

Ruth blushed. "Do I?"

"Take a look," said Nessa.

Ruth turned to the mirror and her eyes nearly popped out of her head. "Is that me?"

"Sure is, babe," grinned Nessa and gave the other beautician the thumbs-up. "Nice job, Trace."

When we got back on the bus, no one recognised us.

Nessa had pulled some clothes out of a chest at the back of the salon and Ruth was now dressed in a pink, ripped one-shoulder T-shirt with the words "Goddesses Rule Okay" written on it, and a fab pair of white jeans, as well as pink trainers with silver stars on the side.

She'd given me a pale blue T-shirt with the words "Bite Me" on it.

Sara Jenkins did a double-take when she finally recognised us and nudged Mercedes who was sitting next to her. Mercedes glanced over and her eyes widened with shock.

"It's the ugly duckling," she said.

I made my arms float up like a ballet dancer about to fly. "Yes, but now I'm a swaaaannnnn!" I said as I flew past and took a seat at the back of the bus.

"More like a duck," said Sara sulkily.

And in that moment, I understood something unbelievable. She was jealous.

Tasha turned round and smiled at me. "You look fab, Gemma," she said. "And so do you, Ruth. Really pretty."

"Thanks," I smiled as I did my best to look modest.

Maybe being a Zodiac Girl had its pluses after all.

Chapter Nine
Clear as mud

After a supper of shepherd's pie and peas on Saturday evening, I went out to retrieve my phone from the rubbish area outside. I really wanted to thank Hermie for the makeover vouchers. They'd worked wonders, not only with the way I looked but also with the way people treated me. It had been brilliant when I got back to school; I'd been the centre of attention and felt like a star.

When I got outside the kitchens, to my horror, it looked like the bins had been recently emptied. All that was in one bin was a heap of broken eggshells and a pile of potato peelings. As I was scrabbling about, head in the bin, bum in the air, I heard someone call my name. *Oh no*, I thought as I almost toppled in. *Please don't let Sara or Mercedes have seen me again.*

"Gemma," the voice called again. "I know you're in there."

I swung my legs back down and turned. It was

Hermie, standing with a big grin on his face. He was holding my phone.

"Looking for this?"

I felt sheepish. "Yes. Sorry. I threw it out when I was cross with you."

"You're going to have to stop rummaging about in bins, you know," he said, "or you'll get a reputation as a has bin."

"Oh, ha-ha," I said. "Very funny."

"So the fact that you're looking for the phone, does that mean you're not cross with me anymore?"

I nodded. "Yes. I mean no. Not cross. I wanted to thank you. We had a really good time with Nessa."

"I can see," he said. "You look great. I told you Venus was well aspected. Happy now?"

I nodded again. "Yes… but…"

"But?"

"But… well, it was really cool getting all the nice comments and stuff when we first got back and everyone wanted to talk to me and find out where I'd had my hair done, but…"

"But?"

"But then they all went off, back into their little groups of friends. And Ruth hated the attention and scuttled back upstairs and here I am on my own again. I look great, but it hasn't really made any difference. I feel like Cinderella with no ball to go to."

"Friends take time," said Hermie gently.

"I know. I miss mine. And…"

"And?"

"And even though it was great to be made to look my best, I want people to like me for me, not because I've got a cool haircut. Your grandfather said something like that to me before we went to the salon. Told me to be myself and learn to love myself."

Hermie chuckled again. "Did he now? Sounds like the sort of thing he comes out with. Yeah. Be yourself. Hard lesson, but then that's what Grandpa is all about. And he's right, learn to love yourself – but it doesn't mean you have to go around looking like the back end of a bus, babe. Part of loving yourself is looking after yourself. And Grandpa could definitely do with a haircut."

I laughed and we went to sit on a wooden bench under the copper beech tree to the right of the bins.

"How you settling in otherwise, Gemma?"

"Not sure. This week has been… different… for all sorts of reasons. Not sure if I want to stay."

"Early days," said Hermie. "Don't give up. You're not a quitter. I know from your chart that it's a hard time for you at the moment. Some heavy aspects. A real turning point but you could do something good here. It's all in your horoscope."

"Yeah, I got your message. How can you know all

that? Just who are you really? And one month to make my mark. But how? One week is already over. What does it *really* mean to be a Zodiac Girl?"

"It means what you make it."

"Hermi*eeeee*! What does *that* mean?"

"It means that life can throw all sorts of things at you, but it's what you make of it that matters. Like the way Nessa made you look the best – she was only bringing out what was already there. It's all about choices. Win or quit, sink or swim, gorgeous or frump, goddess or geek."

"You're talking in riddles."

"No, I'm not. Life is what you make it. Choice. Choice. Choice. Can't say it enough times…"

"Er… you can actually," I said, but I think he knew I was joshing him.

"Some people hide away…" he continued.

"Like Ruth."

"Yeah. Like Ruth. Others get out there and rise to all the challenges, ride all the difficulties. Take flight or fight. We both know what you do normally."

"Yeah, normally, I fight or swim or whatever. But this week has been anything but normal. I feel like I lost sight of my self lately. Although… Gemini, that's the sign of the twins, isn't it?"

Hermie nodded.

"Well, maybe that's it," I said. "I have one twin who

has mad hair and is moody and over-sensitive and the other has nice hair and is a fighter. So I'm both, the one who fights *and* the one who runs away. The one who swims *and* the one who sinks. It's not easy having multiple personalities, you know."

Hermie laughed. "Everyone has days when they feel like running away. But maybe now it's time to let the fighter twin have a say." He got up and went over to his bike. "Be the fighter you naturally are. Your chart is not the chart of someone who takes anything lying down. Your chart says you're a winner, and for this one month, heavy aspects, lessons to be learnt and all, you *can* make things happen. It's a real special time for you. Anyway, got to go. Got messages to deliver. Stay cool."

As he rode away, I stared after him. He was a strange person. Kind one minute, up and restless the next. But appearing out of the blue sometimes, like a guardian angel or fairy godmother. *Most peculiar*, I thought as my phone bleeped.

It was the man himself.

"Forgot to say. The Outreach programme," Hermie said. "There are a lot of lonely people out there who need friends, and not just in schools."

"What do you mean?"

"Lady of the Beasts, you'll figure it out."

I raced back upstairs to find Ruth.

"Hey Ruth, can I look at your book on the gods and goddesses?"

"Sure," she said and pulled a heavy book down from her shelf onto the bed.

I sat on her bed and looked up the index at the back. I soon found the page I wanted.

"You were right, Ruth," I said. "Saturn, sometimes known as Cronus. Often depicted in mythology as an old man. Saturn is the taskmaster. That's another way of saying the giver of lessons, isn't it? Sound familiar?"

"Sounds exactly like Dr Cronus," said Ruth looking over my shoulder. "Look up Mercury."

I flicked back through the pages then read. "Mercury, also known as Hermes. Omigod. And listen to this. Grandson of Saturn."

We both looked at each other.

"Mercury. The planet of communication, often portrayed as the winged messenger," said Ruth, reading the rest of the page.

"And Hermie is a motorbike messenger boy," I said.

"And Nessa is?" asked Ruth breathlessly.

"Exactly what I was thinking. Goddess of love and beauty. Hermie said Venus was well aspected in my chart and next thing we know, we meet Nessa. Coincidence or what? She runs a beauty salon and she looks like a goddess. Venus. Nessa could be a nickname for Venus."

"Yeah… maybe," said Ruth.

"Yes, maybe," I said. "And she cracked up when I said that she was a star. Said it was a private joke. Just who are these guys?"

"Call Hermie and ask," said Ruth.

"I will. Mercury rules Gemini. Mercury is the guardian of all Geminis. This is too weird. What sign are you, Ruth?"

"Taurus but that doesn't mean that I'm a Zodiac Girl."

I went back to the book. "Taurus is ruled by Venus. You really got on with Nessa, didn't you?"

Ruth nodded. "I liked her. And I felt she genuinely liked me. She was kind to me. I felt safe with her."

"Could it be…? Do you think that maybe she's really Venus, here on earth in bodily form?"

Ruth looked doubtful. "Dunno. There's got to be a rational explanation. It could be something really simple. People choose names for all sorts of reasons. All names have other meanings – like mine, Ruth, means compassion."

"And my name means gem or jewel. I remember my mum said she picked it because I was like a jewel in her life. Soppy, huh?"

Ruth smiled. "Yeah, but sweet. Maybe the fact that Hermes and Cronus are the names of planets doesn't mean anything. They're just names. Doesn't mean anything. Maybe their family are into planets and stuff like other families are into football and call all the kids after famous football players. It might not mean anything."

"Yeah, I guess," I agreed. *That explanation makes sense,* I thought, but something was niggling me. There was something strange about it all. I was sure there was more to it than a coincidence over names. Ruth was clearly thinking the same.

"Do you think they could be, like, guardian angels, or something?" she asked.

I laughed. "I wondered that. But Hermie isn't the guardian-angel type. He has tattoos."

"So?" asked Ruth. "Who says what they should look like? In my books, it says that the ancient people always used to believe that the planets and stars took human form. Like, Zeus, king of the gods, supposedly lived on a mountain in Greece. I mean, when you think about it, we don't really know who anybody is, do we? There might be loads of people walking around who are more than just people."

My brain was beginning to spin. "You've been reading too many books."

"I guess," said Ruth. "But we don't know a lot about who we really are, do we? I remember my gran always used to say that there are old souls on this planet and young souls. She said the young souls were usually the stupid ones, like yobs who cause trouble. Whenever we'd see a fight between drunks or something on the news, she'd say, 'Huh, it's clearly *their* first time on the planet.' So if there can be old souls and new souls, maybe there can be people who are from the planets. I mean, none of us know where we've come from anyway, do we?"

I laughed. "In that case, I'd say you're an old soul and Sara and her mates are new souls. But who knows? There are so many things I don't understand. Like this whole Zodiac thing. I haven't got a clue what it's really about."

"Ask Hermie," suggested Ruth. "If he is the real Hermes, then he's supposed to be the great communicator. So get him to communicate."

I pressed his number and got through a moment later.

"Hey, Hermie. I have to know, what does it mean to be a Zodiac Girl?"

"You asked that already and I told you – what you make it."

"You *told* me *that* already."

"Okay, then. Different things to different girls," said Hermie. "Depends on the circumstances. Depends on the individual."

"That's so vague, Hermie. It doesn't mean anything."

"Maybe not at the moment. And to tell the truth, some girls have been Zodiac Girls and not done a thing with the opportunity. Others have gone on to do great things. Like Joan of Arc. She was a Zodiac Girl. Madame Curie. What do you think got her started?"

"What?"

"She was a Zodiac Girl and she went for it, big time. Most of the great heroines in history. All Zodiac Girls."

"So why isn't Ruth a Zodiac Girl?"

"Not her turn. It's not in her chart at the moment. You never know. Her time may come later."

"So what am I meant to do?"

Hermie shook his head. "You'll figure it out. I can only tell you the influences that you're under this month."

"I don't know what you mean. Why can't you do magic or something and make it really clear?"

Hermie chuckled. "The magic's all around you, Gemma – just open your eyes. This planet you're on. It's a three-dimensional light show with a million smells, sounds, tastes and feelings. It hangs, a jewel in deep space, turning on its axis each day. What could be more magical than that? And a sun that shines down on us, the moon, the stars, a sky that goes on and on for light years? What more could you want?"

"I don't know. Someone to make sense of it all."

"Gemma, relax. This time is yours, your chance to

make your mark. Be yourself. Be your best self. Go along with the Outreach programme. The way will become clearer."

It feels as clear as mud at the moment, I thought as he clicked off.

Chapter Ten

Chiron House

On Sunday, as half the school went into rehearsals, Ruth and I got ready to go to Chiron House for our first visit on the Outreach programme. We trooped down the stairs to join the group of volunteers waiting in the hall, and I felt a stab of envy as I saw all the other girls excitedly on their way to rehearse *Bugsy*.

"Now I want you all to be on your best behaviour," said Mrs Blain as she led us down the school drive. "And be particularly nice, as one of them is one of our school's main benefactors. We don't want to upset her, do we?"

"No, Miss," we all chorused back.

"I'm not sure I'll know what to do," said Ruth. "I've never done anything like this before."

"It'll be fine," I said. "Like with my gran, she likes to ramble on about her youth or her operations. It'll be no biggie. Just listen patiently, nod now and then, and you probably won't need to say anything. You could even wear your iPod for all they know. Okay?"

Ruth smiled and gave me the thumbs-up. But she didn't look so sure as Chiron House loomed into sight in front of us.

"Wow. It's amazing in here," whispered Ruth as we walked into the reception room and took in the heavy curtains, acres of plush cream carpets and displays of flowers that looked like they would cost most of my pocket money for a year.

"I know," I whispered. "It's like a five-star hotel, only better. No expense spared. They must be very rich old ladies to be in a place like this."

"Well Mrs Blain did say that one of them was a big time benefactor of the school," said Ruth. "Hope I don't get her. I'm bound to put my foot in it."

Across the reception area, Mrs Blain was talking to a sour-faced woman with thinning ginger hair, who was dressed in a pristine white uniform.

"She looks like a bundle of laughs, not," I said nudging Ruth.

Ruth glanced over and suppressed a giggle.

The woman turned towards us and shot us an icy smile.

"Welcome, girls," she said. "I'm Matron and my ladies are expecting you, but before we go in, I want to outline the rules. One," she flicked a bony finger and narrowed her eyes. "No raised voices, *ever*. Two," and another digit was wagged in front of our noses. "No running about, *ever.*"

I threw a quick glance at Ruth but she seemed to be hypnotised by the perfectly manicured red talons on the end of the two fingers wagging close to her face.

Then a third finger stabbed the air, "And three. Stay in the sitting room. No wandering off anywhere under any circumstances. *Ever.* Any questions?"

Who does she think we are? I thought. *A bunch of children?*

Ice Matron gave me a laser look as if she'd read my mind.

"Right, line up here," she barked and proceeded to meticulously inspect our hands. "Hmm. They seem reasonably clean," she said, sounding disappointed.

Once we'd been given the okay, she led us down a long corridor lined with portraits of scowling women.

"Hope we don't meet them," I whispered to Ruth who snorted loudly. Matron stopped in her tracks and asked her if she was unwell.

"I'm fine, Matron. J... just a frog in my throat," she blustered.

"Well, make sure it stays there. I want nothing upsetting my ladies," said Matron, arching one eyebrow.

"I've heard of the ice maiden and the ice man, but now here cometh the ice matron," I whispered, making

Ruth laugh again.

Matron opened a set of glass double-doors and we filed silently through to meet our ladies. One of them I recognised as the lady I'd met briefly in Pentangle and she gave me a smile when I waved at her. There were eight others slumped in vast chintzy armchairs around the room. They looked like a collection of wizened rag dolls. Some were reading, one in the corner was knitting, but most were just staring into space. *God, they look so bored,* I thought. *Like zombies in a five-star prison.*

Matron began to allocate each of us a lady.

"You, off to see Mrs Hamilton," she said to Ruth, pointing her in the direction of the lady from the hairdressers, "That's her in the corner there."

Next, Rose, Imogen and Grace got their ladies, then Matron looked down her nose at me.

"Now you," she said, looking at me as if I was some nasty bacteria. "Name?"

"Gemma Whiting, Miss."

"Don't you 'Miss' me, young lady," she snapped. "Call me Matron."

I had to suppress a giggle as I imagined her saying, "Call me sir."

"Right, Miss Whiting, you can go to Mrs Compton-Grime," she said, nodding towards a small plump lady who was studying a knitting pattern.

She must be well into her eighties, I thought as I studied the old lady's wiry white hair, bullfrog eyes and thin red lips.

"Hello," I said with a smile as I approached her and looked around for somewhere to sit. "I'm Gemma."

She didn't look up.

"Um… is there anything I can do for you?"

"Yes. Bugger off," she said and clicked her needles viciously.

"Pardon?" I asked, hardly believing what I had just heard.

"You heard me. Bugger off. I don't want anyone near me, especially an annoying little brat like you."

But I haven't even done anything to be annoying, I thought. I didn't know what to do or say next, so I looked around to see if anyone else had got a similar rejection. But no, everyone else seemed to be getting on fine, and Mrs Hamilton and Ruth appeared to be having a real laugh together.

"Um…" I began again.

"What! You're still here?" snapped Mrs Compton-Grime, finally looking up. "Can't you see I'm busy?"

"Er, yes, I've come… I'm with…"

"Spit it out, girl. Don't they teach you how to speak properly at your school?" she growled.

"Yes. I mean…"

"What, pray, brings you here to disturb this

sanctuary of peace and quiet?"

"Part of the Outreach programme at school. We visit people. Do good, sort of thing."

"Why?" she asked, staring at me over her thick round glasses.

Good question, I thought. *Maybe I should have taken the part of the undertaker in* Bugsy. *Anything would be better than this.*

Mrs Blain had spotted my situation and came rushing over.

"Everything all right?" she asked.

"No," said Mrs Compton-Grime. "This nasty child is very irritating. Please take her away."

I looked helplessly at Mrs Blain.

"But… but… but…" I stammered.

"Remove her from my presence, NOW!"

Her raised voice caused Matron to look over and scowl at me.

"Come on, Gemma," said Mrs Blain. "Mrs Compton-Grime doesn't want to be visited today. Why don't you go and join Ruth with Mrs Hamilton."

I couldn't move fast enough and was soon on the other side of the room. *Now I've blown it*, I thought. Judging by the way Mrs Blain was fussing over Mrs Compton-Grime and apologising, she was clearly the school benefactor.

Mrs Hamilton smiled up at me. She pulled a cushion

out from behind her back and threw it on the floor.

"Take a perch," she said. "Sorry we don't have enough chairs to go round, but you're a young thing, you'll be okay on the carpet."

I dutifully sat at her feet, next to Ruth.

She leant over close to my ear. "Don't you worry about that old battleaxe," she whispered.

"She said I was annoying," I said. "And I'd hardly opened my mouth."

"Silly old cow," said Mrs Hamilton, reaching out for a gold box next to her chair. "Just because she's old, it doesn't mean she's nice. Here, dear, have a chocolate. Some things never change, you know. Like you have those mean girls at your school. Same in here. There are the good, the bad and the ugly everywhere."

"Tell me about it," I sighed, as I helped myself to a Belgian caramel cream.

And she did. She was hilarious. She told us all about the other "inmates" as she called them, and how one had a habit of leaving her teeth in the fridge overnight so that they were cool in her mouth in the morning. Another was a sleepwalker who regularly had to be rescued from the rose bushes in the garden, and one night from the fishpond. Another unfortunate lady thought the matron was her daughter and kept asking her if she had swallowed something nasty, as she always looked so sour. She also called Matron "Betty" which she didn't like as her name was Marjorie.

After half an hour of hilarious stories, she said, "Right, now it's your turn. Tell me all about school."

We bombarded her with tales of the bonkers teachers and the yucky school food and our fellow pupils' foibles. I even told her about Sara and her mates, and how mean they could be, but how I'd answered back a few times. Mrs Hamilton seemed to lap it all up and laughed out loud so often that the Ice Matron came over to see if she was all right. By the time we had to leave, I felt like we were old friends.

"Do come again," she said squeezing my hand when I got up to go. "I've really enjoyed today, and meeting you and Ruth. I only arrived last week and I'm bored out of my mind already. I enjoy a good laugh and they are few and far between around here." Then she winked and said, "I guess the problem is, it's full of old people."

"Not you, though," I said and winked back.

"Is there anything we can bring you next time?" asked Ruth.

"Oh, anything to liven the place up a bit. I'm sure you'll think of something. We're not dead yet, you know, but the way we get treated, sometimes you'd think we were."

Chapter Eleven
Planet Deli

The following week, I began to feel more confident about finding my way around school and finding where my classes were. I buried my head in schoolwork and tried not to think any more about friends and whether or not I was liked. I also chose to ignore the strains of *Bugsy Malone* that echoed in the school corridors every night as everyone in the show went into rehearsal mode. Instead, I tried to focus on what was good in my life. Ruth was beginning to open up and I found that beneath her shy appearance was a sweet and generous person. So she wasn't like Jess and my old friends – but then, no one could ever take their place.

Every day I checked the site to see if Hermie had sent anything interesting for my second week as a Zodiac Girl, but there was nothing there that made much sense to me. Just a list of predictions that could have been written in Greek for all the sense they made to me.

Monday: Mercury and Pluto are in a rare state of harmony.

Well, hurrah for them, I thought, but the day did go smoothly and Rose, Imogen and Grace asked me to be on their team in a history quiz. And Tasha moved over in assembly so that I could take my place next to her. Sara didn't look too happy about that, though.

Tuesday: The Moon is well aligned with Jupiter, resulting in a fruitful time.

There was fruit salad after supper, so maybe it meant that.

Wednesday: The Sun is linked to Uranus, so expect the unexpected.

I slipped on a newly washed floor on the way to maths. That was unexpected. I felt a right twit.

Thursday: Saturn and Mercury form an uneasy alignment.

I did have a run-in with Sara when she asked me where my pet mouse was, meaning Ruth. I told her that I didn't have a pet mouse, but I had seen a rat coming out of her room yesterday. It wasn't a very pleasant encounter.

Friday: Another harmonious line-up with Pluto and the Sun.

It was an okay day. In the afternoon, Mrs Blain gave us a run through of our duties for the next visit to Chiron House and told us to think of something we could take, but that was all.

Saturday: Jupiter is in a generous mood.

Bully for him, I thought, as I got ready to go into the village with Ruth for our weekly outing.

"My parents sent me some money," she said with a shrug as we went down for the bus. "Guilt money. So let's go and spend it!"

"Cool," I said. "Jupiter rocks I guess."

Ruth gave me one of her you're-a-very-strange-person looks, but I could tell she was starting to like me more. She didn't hide in her books as much anymore and sometimes even said as much as two sentences.

"Zodiac messages," I said by way of explanation. "Jupiter is in a generous mood, apparently. I still don't quite know what to make of it all, though. Like, is this it? Went to a goddess workshop, got my hair done and

117

got some fab products to keep it straight. Then Hermie said to join the Outreach programme and although it was nice meeting Mrs Hamilton, I can't help thinking, so what? Is that all I get to achieve as a Zodiac Girl? A volunteer with nice hair who visits old people's homes?"

"It's only been two weeks," said Ruth. "Maybe the best is yet to come."

Or the worst, I thought. The first two weeks hadn't exactly been smooth sailing.

We had a lovely afternoon, though, cruising the shops and trying on clothes and make-up and Ruth insisted on paying for treats like hot chocolate and sweet pastries in a Greek deli off the high street. We chose it out of all the other cafés because it was called Europa, like our house back at school. I felt bad about Ruth forking out for everything because I didn't have a lot of pocket money and wanted to spend what I did have on phone vouchers to call my old mates, but Ruth didn't seem to mind.

"What else am I going to do with the money?" she grinned as she tucked into her pastry. "Just call me Jupiter."

"Oh *noooo*," I groaned. "Don't tell me that you're one of them as well."

"Nope," she said, then made her eyes go cross-eyed. "Just me. Quite normal."

At that moment, the deli owner came over with a plate of sumptuous-looking cakes that he put in front of us.

"On ze house," he said with a Greek accent as he stroked his expansive belly and smiled. "Eat. *Eat*. I'm in a generous mood today."

I couldn't resist. "Your name's not Jupiter by any chance, is it?"

He looked taken aback but he quickly recovered then laughed. "Most people call me Joe but if you want call me Jupiter, iz fine by me."

After he'd gone, I nudged Ruth. "Did you see the apron he was wearing?"

Ruth nodded. "Same pattern as Hermie's tattoo."

"And Dr Cronus's tie and Nessa's earrings," I said.

"And the deli is called Europa, which as we know from school is…"

"One of the four moons of Jupiter!" I finished for her.

Ruth looked over at the friendly deli man. "Hmm. Joe – Jupiter. I wonder if he's one of them too? Wouldn't mind having him as my guardian if he is. Look at all the cakes."

I laughed. "Yeah. Slightly more appealing than a guy with tattoos and a motorbike."

"Talking of which," said Ruth. "Eyes left."

Hermie had just parked his bike outside. He entered the deli a moment later.

"Hi," he called to Joe, then turned to us. "I see you've met my dad then?"

Ruth and I looked at each other and almost choked.

"How many planets are there in astrology?" I asked Hermie as he sat at the table next to us.

"Ten," said Joe bringing a plate of ham-and-cheese rolls over to give to Hermie. "Sun, Moon, Venus, Mercury," he winked at Hermie at this point, "Jupiter, Mars, Neptune, Saturn, Uranus and Pluto."

"And could it… is it possible… do you think that maybe those planets might be here in human form?" I asked. "Like in the old days in ancient Greece?"

Joe stroked his chin. "Veeeery interesting question," he said then turned to Hermie. "This is your Zodiac Girl, yes?"

Hermie nodded.

"Bright kid," said Joe then went back behind the counter where he looked like he was chuckling to himself.

"So?" I asked Hermie.

"So what?" he replied.

"So are you guys embodiments of the planets or not?"

"Complicated. Not exactly that simple," he said, then grinned, put his arm out and flexed his muscles. "Though people do say that I have a heavenly body."

Joe cracked up laughing behind the counter.

"So are you going to tell me anything?" I insisted.

Hermie shook his head. "Maybe. What would you like to hear?"

I felt like throttling him. He never gave me a direct answer.

"*Anything.*"

"Only got one message for you today, chick," he said. "Mercury is going to go retrograde for a week."

"Meaning?"

"Mercury is the planet of communication, so when it goes retrograde there are often mix-ups with communications. Misunderstandings. Computers crashing. Technology breaking down. Messages misplaced. Thought I'd better come and tell you before it all started happening."

"But is it going to be a good or a bad week?"

"Depends what you make of it," he said as he wolfed down his sandwich, then got up to go. "Anything could happen."

"Hermieeeeeeee! You're doing it again. Being vague. Not really telling me *anything.*"

Hermie smiled a kilowatt smile. "You'll be fine. Just keep fighting and never give up. Going retrograde, it's nothing to worry about... I don't think. As I told you before, life is what you make of it. Catch you later."

Somehow I didn't feel reassured.

Chapter Twelve
Lady of the Beasts

"Omigod," I heard Mercedes say as Dad's old van chugged its way up the drive. "Have you seen the state of that?"

I went and stood close to her in the courtyard where a crowd of girls were waiting for their parents. I was only expecting Dad, as Mum had phoned early that morning to say she couldn't make it. She'd come down with some flu bug and sounded dreadful.

"I know. It's marvellous isn't it?" I said. "Vintage model. *Very* rare. Only one left in the whole world."

Tasha laughed but in a nice way. She was laughing *with* me, whereas Sara, Mercedes and Lois were always laughing *at* me.

"And have you seen that *thing* in the front?" sneered Sara.

I looked over at the van. Sitting in the passenger seat, with his nose out of the window, was the best sight I'd seen all week.

"Bertie!" I cried.

Sara rolled her eyes up to the sky. "You'd better not bring that disgusting thing anywhere near me," she said. "I'm allergic to animal fur and he looks like he needs a bath."

"Bertie's very clean," I said. "And he's not a thing, he's a dog."

Bertie looked in my direction and yelped with delight. Dad opened the door for him and, with his tail wagging madly, he shot over to me and tried to jump up into my arms.

"He looks a bit like you. Is he your brother?" asked Sara. "I can see the family resemblance with all that mad hair."

I'd had enough. There was no reason for her to be so horrible to me, and I'd done my best to be friendly to her and her mates. I'd decided that I wasn't going to put up with it any longer. *Be yourself*, Dr Cronus had said. *Be the fighter you naturally are*, Hermie had said. I was going to be that. The fighter. I never used to let people walk all over me at my previous school, but I had lost myself for a while when I'd arrived at this one. Thanks to Ruth and Nessa and Hermie, I'd found myself again. And I'm not the victim type. I am a Zodiac Girl, the Lady of Beasts. *Grrr*.

I leant on one hip and looked at her with pity. "Sara, he's a *dog*. A D.O.G. Haven't you ever seen one before, or are you stupid? Who in their right mind

123

would actually think that he's my brother? That's pathetic. But maybe I shouldn't embarrass you. It can't be your fault that you haven't got one brain cell in that empty head of yours. In fact, your head is so empty that if someone shone a torch in your ear, your eyes would light up."

Sara's jaw dropped. She went red, and for a moment looked lost for words.

"Get lost, er… er… pig for… er…" she managed to finally stutter.

"Pig for what, Sara?" I asked. "For breakfast? For lunch? For brains? Come on, spit it out. What are you trying to say?"

"Oh, never mind," said Sara and flounced off with Lois.

Mercedes linked arms with Tasha. "Well, you might have had your hair done," she said. "But you still haven't got any friends here."

"Yes, I have," I said. "I have Ruth." I was beginning to like Ruth. She wasn't exactly the life of the party like my old mates, but she was a gentle soul and there was something about her that made me want to look after her. Like this morning, I felt really sorry for her. As her parents were abroad on a year's contract, she wouldn't be having any visitors. I invited her to spend the day with Dad and me but she shook her head and said she'd be in the way and nothing I could do would reassure her that she wouldn't be. But she looked so small and sad curled up on her bed on her own.

"Pfff," said Sara, turning back. "That mouse."

"Better than being a cow like some people," I said.

Sara looked shocked but Tasha looked like she was going to laugh. As Mercedes pulled Tasha away, I noticed that Tasha yanked her arm out of her grasp. As she did, she turned back to me and mouthed, "Sorry."

Dad soon joined Bertie, and I gave him the grand tour of the school and filled him in on my first two weeks. The edited version. I'd been thinking a lot since the day before and wasn't so sure that I wanted to leave anymore. I was feeling stronger. Better. I wanted to give it a while longer. And it wasn't only because I'd had a makeover. It did feel fab to look better and have some admiring looks and comments, but it was still the same me, straight or frizzy hair. Milk-bottle glasses or cool ones, it was still me inside looking out of them. I didn't want people to like me because I looked okay. I wanted people to like me because of who I am. Inside. Suddenly it didn't seem such a big deal that I hadn't got in with Sara and Co. I wondered why I'd been so bothered about what they thought. I didn't even *like* them, although I was beginning to think that Tasha might be okay if she wasn't with Sara.

There were other girls in the school who weren't unkind. It might take some time to get to know them all, but I didn't want to quit just because some mean girls had picked on me.

After the tour, we had coffee and Danish pastries in the dining room with the other visitors. As we were eating, Dad's mobile rang so he got up to take the call.

"Gemma," he said when he came back moments later, "would you mind if I left you for a couple of hours? I can pop back later to have tea with you. It's just that there's been an emergency and I'm the nearest. A car's broken down on the motorway and they need road rescue. It's only fifteen minutes from here, so I could pop out, sort them out then be back."

"I could come with you," I said. I wanted to spend as much time as possible with him, but he wasn't listening. He was scanning the room for someone.

"Hey, where's Bertie?" he asked.

"Maybe asleep under a table somewhere. You know what he's like."

We searched all the spots where he could possibly have hidden, but he was nowhere to be found.

"Oh dear," said Dad as he looked at his watch. "I have to get going soon. I can't leave people stranded by the roadside. I hope Bertie's not got into any mischief. Where *is* he?"

We decided to split up to search for him and I offered to do the gardens. It had started raining outside so I went upstairs to get a jacket. When I opened the bedroom door, Ruth glanced up and beamed at me. There, sitting in her lap, was Bertie, and he and Ruth looked like the oldest of old pals.

"He's gorgeous," she said as Bertie gave her face a lick. "I knew it was him from your picture.

"But where…? How did he get up here?"

"I went down to get a drink at tea time and to avoid seeing everyone, I went through the drama department. I thought I heard Sara and her mates coming so I hid in the props department until they'd gone past and there he was asleep on top of a pile of costumes. I brought him up here and… I think he likes me."

"He almost gave my dad a heart attack," I laughed. "Dad had visions of him in the kitchen nicking tonight's dinner. I had visions of him chasing Boris!"

Ruth shook her head. "No. Nothing like that. He's been very good. He's a really special dog."

As she sat there stroking him, I thought I hadn't seen her so happy in all the time I'd known her. And then something hit me. Suddenly, I knew what it meant that I was the Lady of the Beasts.

"Ruth," I said. "I've just had the *most* brilliant idea."

Chapter Thirteen
Darned dog

Ruth looked horrified. "Keep Bertie here? But you know dogs aren't allowed. Where? How? For how long?"

"We can keep him in here. We can sneak food up to him. It's only for a few hours."

Ruth was shaking her head. "No. We'll get into real trouble."

"I'll take responsibility if we get caught, and it's only until later."

"But why? What difference is a couple more hours going to make?"

"All the difference. Remember the Outreach programme? The visit to Chiron House?"

Ruth nodded. "Yes. I'm going later."

"So am I, now that Dad's out of the way. And remember Mrs Blain said that we had to take something with us when we visit?"

Ruth's jaw dropped. "She meant take a book or a cake or something. Not an *animal*. Not *Bertie!* Are you out of your mind?"

"No. I've never been more certain about anything. It's the right thing to do. I saw a programme on telly over the summer holidays about using animals as therapy. It was amazing. They have astounding results with people in homes. People who never spoke opened up, and others who were very sad became happier, and... and it lowers blood pressure, and good stuff like that."

"But..."

"No buts, Ruth. When I saw you with Bertie just now, it all clicked into place. What I'm meant to do. And I'm sure that this is what Hermie's been hinting about – you know, Lady of Beasts, join the Outreach programme, saying that there are lonely people everywhere, not just in schools. Don't you see? It's *obvious!* He meant the old ladies."

Ruth shook her head but her lack of enthusiasm didn't put me off. I knew taking Bertie to the Old People's home and starting my own animal-therapy programme was what I was meant to be doing. Thanks to Nessa, I now knew that it was my calling as Lady of the Beasts.

"Dad's got to go and do a road rescue so he'll be gone a while. It's too brilliant. Like fate made a car break down so that Dad would have to leave Bertie here. It will be great. If anyone knocks, shove Bertie in the cupboard, and if he barks, cough like mad, as though you've got a terrible chest infection."

Ruth looked horrified. "Woah. Gemma. Calm down. Think this through. I mean, *fate?*"

I felt dizzy with excitement. "Yes! Fate! Destiny is calling. The stars are in place. I am the Zodiac Girl…"

Ruth shook her head. "I think you've gone mad."

"No. Ruth, this is why I *am* the Lady of the Beasts. Don't you see? *Everything* has been leading up to it. I am *meant* to make this happen. To make other people happy through Bertie. Like Joan of Arc. And Madame Curie. They were both Zodiac Girls too. I am meant to comfort the old by taking animals to visit them."

Ruth was still looking at me as though I'd grown an extra head. "But Madame Curie discovered radioactivity and Joan of Arc led France into battle against the English. And then she was found guilty of witchcraft and burnt at the stake."

"Oh… was she? Hmm. Hermie didn't mention that bit. But he *did* say that Zodiac Girls all have a different calling. And I'm sure that this is mine. You needn't worry. No one's going to burn *me* at the stake for this."

Ruth raised an eyebrow, like she thought that was exactly what was going to happen.

Getting rid of Dad was a doddle, as he was eager to get off and do his road rescue. After making me promise to search high and low for Bertie, he said he'd be back later to pick him up. Then he sped off in his trusty old van.

And now it's time for me to do my rescue job, I thought as energy surged through me. I felt like someone had recharged my flat battery. Plugged me into an electricity source. *Be the fighter you are,* Hermie had said. I would. I felt invincible. I would heal the sick, comfort the old, entertain orphaned children, save the whales... Everyone would love Bertie. I'd be a hero and everyone would be happy and both of us would be so popular.

I snuck some pastries up to the room and Bertie wolfed them down in one gulp. Then we waited until it was time to go and visit the home.

"How are you going to get him out?" asked Ruth. "Someone's bound to notice you. Did any other parents bring pets?"

"Ah, no," I said. "But it needn't be a problem. I'll put him in my little wheelie case. But other pets. Hey, good idea Ruth. Next week, I'll put up a notice inviting girls to bring their animals and we can take a whole load down. By then, everyone will have seen how it works so Chiron House will welcome them all."

"Noooo," Ruth wailed. "Gemma, please. Just get today over with."

I saw her point. Maybe it was a bit over-ambitious

to take more than one dog on the first few visits. But I had visions of the future. I would develop my animal-therapy programme so that there would be girls going into old people's homes all over the place, all over the country, all over the world, with their pets.

At two o'clock, Ruth began to get her things ready to go to Chiron House.

"I'll see you there," I said as I stroked Bertie's head. "I'll wheel him down. It's only five or ten minutes down the drive. Tell Mrs Blain that I'm walking down."

"Will she allow you on your own?"

"Course. Look, if you're worried, tell her that I was seeing Dad off. She'll understand when I explain later."

"Okay. But I hope you won't get expelled or anything," she said in her usual worried way.

"Not likely," I said. She really didn't see. I'd probably get a medal, or an article written about me in the paper. Lady of Beasts alive and well and living locally. Then a TV station would pick up on it and I'd be interviewed for the news. And then I'd be a celebrity and… and maybe be taken to London to meet the Prime Minister, maybe even the Queen. I felt brilliant, better than I had in weeks.

After Ruth had gone, I waited in the room for ten minutes, then went down to check that everyone going to the Home had left and that most of the others had gone into *Bugsy* rehearsals.

Once I was certain that they had, I went back up to get Bertie.

I pulled my wheelie case off the top of the wardrobe, put it on the floor and unzipped it.

"In," I commanded as I pointed at the case.

Bertie wagged his tail and jumped on the bed.

"*In*," I said again while still pointing at the case.

Bertie didn't move apart from to keep wagging his tail.

I lifted him off the bed and attempted to put him in the case. Sadly, he thought it was a game, and as soon as I let go, he leapt back on the bed.

I tried again.

"In the case," I said as he tried to lick my face. "In the case."

"Woof," he said and jumped out, then went and hid under the bed with his nose sticking out under the bedspread.

"This isn't a game, Bertie," I said.

"Woof," he said again.

I tried to drag him out, but he wasn't having it and dug his front paws into the carpet.

"I know what will get you out," I said, and went to my drawers to find a biscuit. I got a choc-chip cookie and held it out to him.

He was out like a shot and gulped it down. Then I grabbed him and stuffed him into the wheelie case. *Almost there*, I thought as I began to zip round him. I almost had it done when I realized that his right leg was still out. I let go of his front paws and put his right leg in the case. He stuck the left one out.

"Bertie!" I cried in exasperation. "Just get in the case."

He looked at me quizzically and licked my hand. I grabbed the stray leg with one hand then quickly zipped up the zipper around him with the other hand.

He gave me one of Ruth's what-on-earth-are-you-doing-now? looks as his face disappeared into the case. I left a few inches open so that he could breathe and, quick as a flash, he'd stuck a paw through it and was trying to open it.

"Stay *still*, Bertie," I said as I stuffed his paw back down.

He let out a soft whine, then, at last, seemed to settle in the case.

I opened the door and looked left, then right down the corridor. All clear. I headed for the stairs. I couldn't wheel the case down the stairs, so I lifted it up and staggered down. It was really heavy. Inside the case, Bertie had begun struggling again and his nose was poking out of the opening.

"Stay *in*," I urged him, praying that no one would

come out and see me. Luckily, no one did, so I made it to the bottom of the stairs, then made a dash for the front door.

Outside at the front, I put the case down. *So far so good*, I thought as I hurriedly began wheeling the case down the driveway, trying to look as cool as I could. I'd just reached the end of the courtyard when I heard a voice.

"Whiting!"

I turned to see Dr Cronus coming after me.

"And where do you think you're going?" he asked, looking at my case. "Not running away, are we?"

We running away? *We*? *Omigod. Does he know Bertie's in the case?* For a moment I panicked, then realized that "we" was just a figure of speech. He meant was *I* running away?

"No, sir. Outreach programme, sir," I said. "Mrs Blain asked me to take some books down to Chiron House and they were heavy, so I thought I'd wheel them down."

Dr Cronus narrowed his eyes and scrutinised me closely. I held my breath and hoped that Bertie was doing the same.

"Off you go, then," said Dr Cronus and he turned to go back to the school.

As I began to wheel away, Bertie let out a soft bark as if to say, *Hey, I'm still in here.* I began to fake a coughing fit as Dr Cronus turned back.

"Hayfever, sir," I said.

"In September?"

"It's the eucalyptus, sir. It gets me every time."

Dr Cronus rolled his eyes. "See Matron when you get back."

"Yes, sir, doctor, sir," I said, then I legged it as fast as I could with the wheelie case in tow down the driveway.

Halfway there, the case began to feel really heavy, even though it was on wheels. The distance from the bottom of the drive to Chiron House took a couple of minutes in the car, but by foot, it was another matter. As soon as we were round a corner and out of sight of the school, I unzipped the case, let Bertie out and put him onto his lead.

He was delighted to be out in the open and began to run ahead, dragging me with him. I did my best to keep up with him but he was too strong for me, and in the end, he pulled the lead out of my hand. He raced off down the drive and round the next corner. I chased after him, but as I turned the corner, there was no sign of him.

"Oh *no*," I cried. "*Bertie*. Bad dog. Heel."

Only silence greeted me.

Fifty yards away, I could see Chiron House.

Oh, hell and Horlicks, I thought. *Now what? Now I really have lost Bertie. Dad's going to kill me when he gets back.*

I stood on the driveway not knowing which way to turn. Whether to go back, forward or just lie down and cry.

Dad was right. Darned dog. How could I ever have thought Bertie could comfort the old when he drove the young completely and utterly bonkers?

"BERTIE!!!"

Chapter Fourteen

Oops!

I started to walk back to the school. *Best just go and wait for Dad and tell the truth*, I thought. *No point in going on to Chiron House now. I'd never be able to concentrate.* I felt completely defeated.

As I made my way back up the driveway, I suddenly heard a familiar roar. Hermie!

I turned round to see the most amazing sight. Hermie was riding towards me on his motorbike, and sitting in front of him, paws up on the handlebars and ears blown back, was Bertie. I burst out laughing. They looked so ridiculous.

Hermie pulled up besides me.

"Lose someone?" he asked.

I nodded. "He slipped his lead," I said. "Thanks so much for bringing him back. Bad dog, Bertie."

Bertie turned and gave Hermie a lick.

Hermie grinned and scratched Bertie's ear. "He's very sorry, aren't you, boy? I found him out on the road. He seemed to enjoy the ride."

Bertie raised an ear and barked in agreement.

"But how did you know he was mine?"

Hermie turned his bike round. "He told me, of course," he said. Bertie woofed in agreement then gave Hermie a last lick and jumped off the bike. "Catch you both later." And he blasted off down the drive.

"So now he can communicate with animals as well as everything else?" I said to Bertie as I put him back on his lead then turned to Chiron House. All was not lost. Once again, my hero Hermie had appeared out of the blue to my rescue.

When we reached Chiron House, I knocked on the door and waited a few minutes but no one answered, so I tried the huge brass doorknob to see if it was open. It was, and Bertie and I slipped in. Behind reception was a girl who looked only a few years older than me. She was sitting with her feet up on the desk with her eyes closed and headphones on, so she didn't hear us until we were almost on top of her. When she realized that someone was there, she almost leapt out of her skin.

"Omigod!" she exclaimed as she removed the headphones. "You shouldn't creep up on people like that."

"Oh. Sorry... didn't mean to startle you..."

"So? Waddayawant?"

I made myself stand up tall and look confident. "I'm with the… er… the animal comfort for old folk programme. I… I haven't seen you here before?"

"Yeah. So?" said the girl with a shrug. "I'm standing in for my mum while she's gone to the shops. I think some of your lot have gone in already." She jerked her thumb down a corridor. "Down there. With all the wrinklies."

Phew, I thought. *That was lucky.* I had my story about animal therapy all straight in my head, but I was glad that it had been her at the desk and not Matron.

I led Bertie in the direction that she'd pointed and there, through glass-panelled double swing doors, I could see the ladies having tea and sandwiches. A few of the girls from our school were talking or reading to their ladies, and Ruth was walking around with a tray of teacups.

"Okay, Bertie, destiny awaits," I said as I patted his head and took a deep breath. "It's showtime, folks."

I opened the door and walked in.

"WAGGGGGGGHHHHHHHH!" shrieked Mrs Compton-Grime, her eyes popping out further than usual the moment she spotted Bertie. "Ma*T-ROOOOOON,*" she screeched as she cowered back in her chair. "It's a dog, a nasty *dirty* dog. Get him out of here. Get HIM OUT OF HERE!"

Another of the ladies dropped her teacup, while the

others stared in amazement as Bertie, being the friendly soul that he is, raced over and bounded onto Mrs Compton-Grime's lap, where he started furiously licking her face.

"ARRRGGH SPPLUURGGGG YUCCCHHH," she shouted as she tried to push him off.

Unfortunately, Bertie thought she was playing a game and licked all the harder.

"Smmurfffgruumphhh, off, get *off*," she blustered and finally pushed Bertie off her lap. Suddenly airborne, Bertie managed a quick twist and landed with a soft thump on her knitting basket, knocking it over and creating a multicoloured torrent of wool as balls rolled off in all directions.

Oh hell and Horlicks, I thought as he dived after them. He loves knitting wool as he used to play with it when he was a puppy.

"Not my knitting, *not my knitting*, off, *off*, OFF," cried Mrs Compton-Grime, desperately grabbing at a ball of her wool.

Bertie immediately took this as a sign that another game had begun and tried to pull it out of her hand with his teeth.

I rushed over to try and get him away but he was off, the ball of wool firmly clamped in his mouth.

"NO. *STOOOOOP* HIM," cried Mrs Compton-Grime as she tried to grasp the four-legged rocket, but he was too fast for her and dived under a low table laid for tea. The cups rattled in their saucers and tea slopped a bit, but mercifully the cups stayed upright.

From there, Bertie skidded round another chair and over a sofa. Then he repeated the action in reverse. By now all the girls were chasing him. A jumping, diving, slipping, sliding, laughing mob frantically followed the trail of bright red wool that now covered half the room. The old ladies watched in horrified silence as their tranquil sitting room turned into mayhem and at the centre of the chaos sat Mrs Compton-Grime. Round and round and round her chair ran Bertie until yards of wool had wrapped around her. Trapped by her own knitting wool, she was a prisoner in her own chair and screamed to the high heavens for Matron.

"Ma-*TROOOOOOOOOOOOOOOOOOOOOOOOOON!*"

"Sorry," I said as I made a dive for Bertie. "Oh, I'm so, *so* sorry."

Suddenly the ball of wool ran out and Bertie stopped dead in his tracks – as did his throng of pursuers, who collided with each other and ended up in an untidy pile of arms and legs at Mrs Compton-Grime's feet.

For a second or two there was silence.

Disappointed by the red ball's disappearance, an out-of-breath Bertie flopped on his tummy, legs splayed out on either side of him.

It was time to make my move and I quietly approached him. Slowly I reached out and was about to grab him, when a cat popped its head out from under the sofa. Disturbed from a deep sleep, it had been observing the situation, wisely waiting until the madness stopped before attempting to escape. Unfortunately, it stepped right in front of Bertie, who perked up immediately. *Oh no*, I thought, *chasing cats is another of Bertie's favourite games*.

"Wooff GRRRR. Woof," growled Bertie.

"MeOOWWWWWW," replied the cat.

"Arrrghh," sighed Mrs Compton-Grime and slumped back into her chair as if someone had let all the air out of her.

The cat stopped, arched its back and seemed to double in size as every strand of its fur stood on end.

"Bertie, heel, *heel*," I cried, as everyone in the room looked on in anticipation.

But Bertie wasn't listening. He leapt to his feet and the two stood looking at each other like a couple of gunfighters, eyeball to eyeball, nose to nose. Then the cat made a run for the French windows.

Bertie dashed after it, hitting the low table and sending the teacups, plates and sandwiches flying.

The cat hit the window. It was closed. Bertie skidded into the cat who let out a terrible wail and clawed its way up the curtains. To Bertie, this was a brilliant new twist to the game, so he sank his teeth into the folds of material and began to shake it violently. The cat hung on, digging its claws deeper as the soft velvet spun round and round.

"Maybe we'd better let them out," said Rose, going to the door and unlatching it.

"Noo*oo*," I cried, "not without his lead." But it was too late; she'd done it and the cat shot off into the garden. In the few seconds it took for Bertie to realize that his prey was no longer confined to the curtain, the cat had run halfway across the garden. With a bark of enthusiasm, Bertie spotted it and the chase was on again. Over flowerbeds, around the rose bushes they raced, both getting muddier and muddier. Then the cat made an almighty leap over the high garden wall and it was all over.

After a couple of triumphant barks and a quick scratch, Bertie trotted back over the muddy flowerbeds and re-entered the room where, blind to the scene of complete devastation surrounding him, he began hoovering up the sandwiches and biscuits that lay scattered all over the floor.

At that moment, Matron walked in. "What the…?" she exclaimed after taking in the half-torn-down curtains, the smashed crockery, the upset chairs and tables and finally Mrs Compton-Grime, who was still tied to her chair. Matron's eyes rolled up into the back of her head and she fainted.

Oh nooooooo! I thought. Bertie's *third* favourite game! He loves it when people play dead. He was quick off the mark – in a flash, he was on Matron's chest, attempting resuscitation by pawing her and licking her face with great enthusiasm.

It seemed to work.

She slowly opened her eyes to see a large pink tongue covering her face. Behind this was what appeared to be a small bundle of furry mud, much of which was sticking to her perfect white uniform. She gave a sigh and passed out again.

I pulled Bertie off her as most of the other old ladies, who were clearly anxious about what he was going to do next, cowered behind the sofa. Only Mrs Hamilton seemed to be unfazed by the scene. In fact, she seemed to be highly amused. I gave her an apologetic look as I picked Bertie up and held him tightly in my arms. He gave my cheek a huge lick, as though to thank me for giving him the time of his life.

"We're leaving, we're leaving," I said in an attempt to reassure the worried ladies. "He's harmless, honestly. He won't harm anyone."

"WHO is responsible for this?" asked a stern voice behind me.

I turned to see Mrs Blain, who had just come in from the kitchen carrying a fresh pot of tea.

All eyes turned to me.

What could I possibly say to get out of this? I wondered as her astonished face turned my way.

"Er... oops!"

Chapter Fifteen

Suspension?

The Lady of the Beasts is in the doghouse.

It would be funny if everyone wasn't so cross with me.

Dad hit the roof when he got back and found out what I had done. He apologised profusely to everyone, then made a speedy exit taking Bertie with him.

I called Hermie as soon as I got back to school, but there was no response. In fact, the phone seemed to have gone dead. I tried to check the site but the computer kept crashing and when I finally managed to get online, there was nothing there either except a message confirming what Hermie had said in the deli. Mercury has gone retrograde. The one time I really needed him and he'd done a disappearing act.

Mrs Blain could hardly speak to me, she was so angry. She'd marched me back up to the school and straight in to see Dr Cronus.

"What on earth did you think you were doing?" he asked when she'd explained the situation.

"I was trying to help, sir. I thought some of the old people might like to see a nice pet."

Mrs Blain clucked her tongue at the mention of the words, "nice pet".

"A *nice* pet?" she said. "Is that what you call him? Do you call what he got up to the behaviour of a nice pet? More like a wild beast. The ladies were dreadfully upset and Mrs Compton-Grime looked like she was going to have a heart attack. Not to mention the matron. She had to go home for a lie down. And after all our good work there, now they've threatened to ban us."

Dr Cronus's eyes were boring into me. "Do you realize how this reflects on Avebury, Whiting?"

"Yes, sir. Sorry, sir. I didn't mean to upset anyone. I really… I'm sorry."

"I should think so. Taking a wild dog into an old people's home? You must be insane. There are properly organised programmes for this sort of thing. Programmes where the animals are *trained*."

There was nothing more I could say in my defence so I hung my head, stared at the floor and waited to hear my punishment.

Of course, news of my exploits was all round the school by Monday morning.

"What happened?" asked Rose Watson at

breakfast. "We thought you'd been expelled when you didn't come down last night."

"I was sent to bed early without any supper," I said. "Dr Cronus said I had to reflect on my actions."

Sara and crew suddenly appeared at the end of the table.

"So are you going to get expelled?" asked Sara.

I bet she'd love that, I thought as I took a half-hearted bite of my toast.

"Leave her alone," said Ruth. "Can't you see she's been through enough?"

"Oh, the mouse speaks... or squeaks," laughed Sara, but she did move off.

Tasha, however, lingered behind and sat down opposite me.

Ruth gave her a hard stare as if to say, *Push off.* Tasha leaned over and touched my wrist.

"I'm not going to make fun," she said. "I just wondered what happened. Are they going to expel you?"

I shook my head. "Don't think so. Dr Cronus did say that I came close to it, but as I was a new girl and it was my first offence, I was likely to just get suspended for a week. The teachers are going to discuss my case on Friday and that's when I'll hear. In the meantime, I've been forbidden to go within a hundred yards of Chiron House or I'll be expelled."

"Suspension," said Tasha. "That could be brilliant. It would mean a week at home!"

I shook my head again. Even though a week ago I couldn't wait to get home, I realized that it was the last thing I needed right now, not in these circumstances. A week out and I'd get behind with schoolwork, and I'd never fit in or find friends.

"My parents will kill me. I'd never hear the end of it. And in the meantime, I have to stay in my room every night and I'm not allowed into the common room. I didn't mean to cause trouble. I thought that it must be so boring sitting in that home all day long, and seeing a pet might cheer them up. Bertie's usually so well behaved."

At the table at the far end of the room, Sara, Mercedes and Lois were glaring angrily. Not only at me, but also at Tasha.

"Won't your friends be missing you?" asked Ruth.

Tasha shook her head. "Don't care," she said, then she smiled kindly. "I wanted to check that you were okay. And… and I wanted to say that I'm sorry we… *I've* been mean to you. You didn't deserve it."

I felt my eyes fill with sudden tears. I put my hands up to my face so that no one could see. "Don't be nice to me… You'll… you'll… make me cry."

Tasha laughed. "I thought I made you cry by not being nice to you."

I laughed and Tasha smiled again.

"Do you think, maybe… well, maybe we could be friends?" she asked.

"But Sara and Mercedes…?"

Tasha glanced over at them then pulled a face. "Between you and me, they're not much fun. All they ever seem to do is talk about other people and be horrible about them. It can get a bit wearing, going round with people who are so negative all the time. I thought from day one when we saw you coming out of that broom cupboard that you looked like fun, and I felt really mean when they didn't invite you or Ruth to the sleepover party. Up until now, I guess I felt scared of them, in a way. Like if I went against them, they'd gang up on me as well. And now I don't care. After I saw you stand up to Sara that time outside, I realized I was being cowardly and it was time that I stood up to them as well."

"Good for you," said Ruth, who was beginning to speak out more and more herself.

"Tell us the bit where Bertie tied Mrs Compton-Grime up with her knitting again," said Imogen, coming over from the next table to join us.

The image of Bertie and the wool did make me smile for a moment, although it hadn't seemed funny at the time.

"And the old bird was okay, you know," said Rose.

"As soon as you'd gone, she sat up, right as rain. I think she's an old drama queen who likes to cause trouble."

"That's probably how Sara and her mates will end up," said Tasha. "Bitter old ladies in a home with nothing better to do than grumble and make other people's lives miserable."

"Bertie was out of order, though," I said.

"I guess," said Rose, "but there was no lasting damage done, and Mrs Hamilton said she hadn't had such a good laugh in years and we should all go back as soon as possible."

"Really?" I said. I couldn't believe my ears. Last night, I thought my life was over. The old ladies hated me. The teachers were mad at me. No one at school liked me except Ruth, and yet here I was, surrounded by friendly faces, having breakfast and having a laugh. *Exactly how I'd hoped it would be,* I thought.

On Tuesday evening, Rose and Imogen invited Ruth and me to a sleepover in their room. Everyone wanted to hear the story of Bertie's visit over and over again. Even some of the Year Elevens popped in for a while to sympathise.

"Tough," said Fleur. "Okay, you acted irresponsibly, but you don't deserve to be suspended. Everyone makes mistakes."

On the website, there was still zilch. On the phone, also zilch.

Where are you, Hermie? I wondered as the week went on.

By Friday, I was starting to get seriously worried about my future. Even though I'd been on my best behaviour all week and had done as I was told, the teachers were distant with me, and Mrs Blain, who was usually so friendly, treated me like an outcast.

On Friday afternoon, half our year went off to the rehearsal for *Bugsy* as usual and Ruth was preparing to go to the Outreach programme meeting.

"Are you sure you can't come?" Ruth asked.

I shook my head. "My case comes up this afternoon, so Mrs Blain said to sit this one out until the school has decided what to do with me. She's given me lines to do. What are you going to do at the meeting, now that Chiron House has threatened to ban us?"

"I guess we're going to have to make new plans and find new places to go," said Ruth.

"That's not fair," I said. "I feel so bad, because it wasn't anybody else's fault. I caused the trouble. I feel rotten, especially as I think Mrs Hamilton looked forward to us going."

"I know," said Ruth. "I liked her, but it seems like Mrs Compton-Grime calls the shots round there."

After Ruth had gone to the meeting, I sat down and began my lines.

I will not take pets into old people's homes.

I will not take pets into old people's homes.

I will not take pets into old people's homes.

I wrote the line over and over. By the hundredth line, I was getting bored. I checked my phone, but there was still no message from Hermie, so I went to the astrology site.

There were five messages.

Sorry I've not been in touch, but I've been feeling a bit backwards lately.

Wrongs can be made right.

Nothing is over until it's over.

Keep fighting.

Listen to your inner voice.

Back soon. Hermie XXX

What inner voice? I asked myself. *Isn't listening to inner voices what mad people do?* I decided that I was a bit mad so why not give it a go? I sat quietly, to try and tune in to my inner voice. At first I felt stupid as various thoughts floated through my head.

I wonder what's for supper tonight?

I wonder if I will be suspended, and what I'll say to Mum and Dad? And Gran?

It'd be nice to see Jess and the girls though.

But they'll all be at school, so most of the time I'll be on my own.

Keep fighting. How?

And then it seemed like the floodgates had opened and my inner Gemini twins were having an argument.

Life is what I make it. A disaster so far.

Stay in and do my lines.

Be myself. I'm a fighter.

No, I'm not. I don't want to cause trouble.

Nothing is over until it's over.

I am Lady of the Beasts. Grrrr.

I am the Zodiac Girl. Arghhh.

What should I do?

Stay in my room and lie low.

Go to Chiron House and apologise.

But I'll get expelled.

Go to Chiron House and apologise.

But I'll get into trouble.

Go to Chiron House and apologise.

Go to Chiron House and apologise.

Go to Chiron House and apologise.

Go to Chiron House and apologise.

Go to Chiron House and apologise.

Go to Chiron House and apologise.

It seemed my split personality had merged and the Gemini twins that live in my head agreed on something at last. Either that, or one of them punched the other's lights out.

I had to go to Chiron House and apologise.

I tried to call Hermie and ask what he thought, but the line was still dead, so I pulled my jacket out of the wardrobe and my black woolly hat. I figured that if I pulled the hat down over my head until I got to the home, if any of the teachers saw me creeping off, they wouldn't realize that it was me.

Everyone was in classes when I got downstairs, so I made for the front door, then legged it as fast as I could down the driveway.

I got within a few yards of Chiron House, then panic hit me. What was I doing? Dr Cronus had said that I'd be expelled if I went within a hundred yards of Chiron House and here I was, right outside. Did I really want to be expelled? A week ago, it would have been the answer to all my problems. I'd be back at my old school. I'd be back at home. But now, I didn't want it to happen that way.

I was about to set off back up the path when I saw someone behind the bushes in the back garden of Chiron House.

"WHO'S THERE?" croaked an elderly voice.

I ducked down behind the bushes, hoping that I could still get away. I heard the sound of footsteps shuffling behind me, and before I knew it, someone had poked me hard in the back with a walking stick.

"OW!" I cried before I could stop myself.

"Come out of that bush, whoever you are,"

commanded the voice. "Stand up and show yourself."

Slowly I crawled out and reluctantly stood up, to see Mrs Compton-Grime's angry face staring at me over the hedge.

"You! What on earth are you doing there?" she demanded. "Explain yourself."

"I… I came to apologise," I stuttered.

"Apologise! Herumph," she sniffed. "Bit late for that. I thought I'd told them not to let you within a hundred yards of this place."

"I… I know… I just…"

"No just about it, madam. Clearly you don't know how to follow rules. Now, be off with you. Out of here. And I can tell you, the school will be hearing from me very soon about this matter."

Chapter Sixteen
Hell and Horlicks

Idiot, idiot, idiot, I said to myself over and over as I made my way back up to the school. *Why did I listen to my inner voices? Why did I listen to Hermie? He's only got me into deeper and deeper trouble since day one. I wish I'd never met him. I wish I'd never found out about that stupid site. I wish I wasn't a Zodiac Girl. Now I am going to get expelled.*

As the school came into view, I saw Ruth at the window in the dining room. She waved excitedly when she saw me, then disappeared, only to reappear at the door a few moments later.

"Where have you been?" she asked breathlessly as I got closer. "We've been looking for you everywhere. You won't believe what's happened. Quick, come into the annex."

"Why? What is it?" I asked. "Has someone heard about my punishment?"

"No, nothing like that," said Ruth as she led me to the annex. "Come to the Outreach meeting. You'll soon see."

As we got closer to the annex, I could hear shouting. Mainly from Mrs Blain.

I opened the door and could hardly believe what I saw. It was complete pandemonium. A zoo where all the animals had run wild. And poor Mrs Blain in the middle of it all looking like she was living her worst nightmare.

Rose was there with Boris the cat, who was desperately trying to escape up one of the wooden blinds at the window and was swinging by one paw.

Imogen was holding on to one of the school goats. He was chewing his way through a pile of papers on the teacher's desk.

Grace was busy chasing a couple of hens who were clucking madly, trying to find an exit, and one of them pooped at Mrs Blain's feet.

Alice Jacobs had a cage containing the mice from the science lab and next to her was Marie Wilkinson with a box of frogs, also from the science lab. They gave me the thumbs-up and cheered loudly when they saw me appear at the door.

Hannah Morrison came rushing over, carrying a fishbowl. "I've brought a tadpole," she said. "Um. They don't do much unless you swish the water round."

"And I've brought my imaginary pet," grinned Lucia Peters. "There wasn't anything left by the time

I heard about it, so I had to be creative."

"Heard about what?" I asked. I was mystified. What on earth was going on?

Ruth squeezed my arm. "Revolution," she said. "The girls are revolting."

"Well that's a bit harsh," I said. "I know we didn't like a lot of them in the beginning, but I wouldn't go that far."

"Girls, GIRLS," bellowed Mrs Blain above the din. "QUIETEN DOWN."

The girls became quieter but the animals carried on squawking or meowing or bleating.

"RIGHT," said Mrs Blain above the cacophony. "Who's going to explain this extraordinary display of… of… *outrageous* behaviour?"

Ruth giggled. "It was Tasha's idea," she whispered to me. "She said we had to do something to help you."

"Is SOMEBODY going to tell me what's going on?" demanded Mrs Blain.

Tasha motioned for Ruth to speak up. Ruth went bright red and took a deep breath. "If Gemma gets suspension," she said, "we all get suspension. We've all brought animals for the pet-therapy programme so that Gemma's not the only one."

"Yes," said Tasha. "If Gemma goes, we all go!"

My jaw fell open.

So did Mrs Blain's.

So did the goat's. But for a different reason. I don't think he liked the taste of schoolbooks and he looked like he was going to be sick.

A dark shadow appeared at the door and I turned to see Dr Cronus standing there, taking in the scene in front of him. He had a face like thunder as he looked around.

"If Gemma gets suspended, we all do," said Ruth again, but this time it came out as barely a whisper.

"All of you," said Dr Cronus after a few moments. "In your rooms, NOW. And I don't want to see one of your faces until we have decided your fate."

Oh, God, I thought as I trooped out with the others. If I wasn't up for expulsion when Mrs Compton-Grime had her say, I certainly was after this little episode.

"I'm not sorry," said Ruth later as we sat on the windowsill of our room and stared out at the trees. "I'd do it again if we had the chance."

"Thanks, Ruth," I said, "but I don't want to get you into trouble for something that was my fault. Or the others. I'm going to take the blame."

Ruth laughed. "It was funny, wasn't it? Did you see that hen poop at Mrs—"

"Omigod. Quick, down," I said as I leapt off the sill and pulled Ruth with me.

"What? What?" she said as she fell onto the floor. "What did you see?"

"Car," I said as I knelt up and peeked up to see out of the window.

Ruth knelt up besides me. "What car? Who?"

I pointed down into the courtyard where an old Rolls Royce had just pulled up. In the back seat, I could clearly see Matron's white uniform and the shape of someone next to her, someone with white hair. Ruth knelt up a bit higher as I quickly filled her in on my attempted visit to Chiron House.

"Oh, God," she said. "That's done it."

I ducked down further. "I don't want them to see me. That has to be Mrs Compton-Grime with Matron. What can you see?"

"It *is* Matron," she said. "Definitely. She's getting out and going round to the other door. She's helping someone out… One of the old ladies, I can't see…" she quickly ducked down again. "Matron looked up at the windows."

"It has to be Mrs Compton-Grime with her," I sighed. "Come to demand they take me out. She said she would. And if she is the school's benefactor, that's me gone."

Ruth peeked. "I can't see," she said. "They're going towards Dr Cronus's office. I can only see their backs… oh… but… oh, I am sorry, Gemma."

I rolled over and lay on the carpet. "Hell and Horlicks," I said. "That's definitely me finished."

Chapter Seventeen

Surprise visitor

"Might as well pack my bags, then," I said gloomily as I pulled my case down from the top of the wardrobe.

Ruth sat on the end of her bed and kept offering me chocolate. I didn't have the appetite for it, though. I had a sick feeling in my stomach as I imagined Mum and Dad's disappointment when they heard the news. I felt so guilty. All the hours they'd spent working so they could give me this opportunity, and now it was like throwing it back in their faces. They were bound to think that I'd done it on purpose.

When I was almost done, I sat on the end of the bed ready to hear my fate.

"I'll really, really miss you," said Ruth.

"Me too," I said, then attempted to give her a smile. "In fact, I'll be sorry to leave…"

"Open up the astrology site. See if Hermie has anything to say."

I shook my head and lay back on the bed. "It's all too late."

But Ruth went to the desk anyway, switched on the computer and this time, it didn't crash as she typed in the site address.

Just as it was downloading, we heard a gentle tap on the door.

Ruth got up to open the door. She looked surprised. "Oh. Hi," she said. "Er…"

"Well? Can I come in?" asked a familiar voice.

"Yes, of course, come in. Gemma, look who it is," said Ruth as Mrs Hamilton stepped in and looked around.

She glanced at me then went over to the window. "Ah," she said. "This brings back memories." Then she saw my case on the floor. "Wherever are you going, child?"

I looked at the floor. "Home, I guess. Expelled."

"Ex*pelled?* Whatever makes you say that?"

"Mrs Compton-Grime. I think she's in with Dr Cronus now…"

Mrs Hamilton sat on the bed and motioned me to sit up next to her. "Tell me everything," she said as she patted my hand.

She listened patiently as I told her my whole mad, sad story.

"… so you see, they're bound to ask me to leave," I sighed as I finished.

"Nonsense," she said.

"*Nonsense*? How can you say that? After what I've done…"

Mrs Hamilton smiled. "Nothing compared to what I got up to when I was here!"

"But… I saw Mrs Compton-Grime arrive with Matron. And… and I think she's a benefactor of our school and what she says goes… and she said… What? You were a pupil here?"

"I was," Mrs Hamilton smiled. "And never mind what Mrs Compton-Grime said. It was me who arrived just now with Matron. And it's *me* who's the school's benefactor. Mrs Compton-Grime hasn't got two pennies to rub together. She just likes to pretend that she's very grand."

"So… so… what's going to happen…?"

But Mrs Hamilton was up again. She'd seen the website on my computer and sat at the desk.

"What's all this?" she asked.

"Ah…" I said. That was the part I'd omitted from the story. "It's… er… it's an…"

"An astrology site," said Ruth.

Mrs Hamilton stared at the screen for a few moments, then at me in amazement. "You're a Zodiac Girl? You *are*, aren't you?" She looked back at the screen. "Oh, this explains everything! Oh, this is *marvellous*. In my day, I got my messages by post, and what a slow process it was. But *this*, of *course*, the Internet…"

"In your day?" I asked. "What do you mean? How did you know I was a Zodiac Girl?"

She pulled out a pendant from underneath her blouse. It was a tiny silver Zodiac symbol on a chain, similar to mine. "Because I was one!" she grinned as she showed us her pendant. "The water-bearer, see? I'm an Aquarian, so that's my symbol. *I* was a Zodiac Girl. Oh, this is too marvellous. I've never met another one before. I knew that there were others out there, but I never knew when or where."

I nodded. "But... how...?"

Mrs Hamilton shrugged. "Been going on for centuries apparently..."

"I know, Joan of Arc. Madam Curie," I said.

"Yes. I was told that. But they managed to do more... er... good than I did. So. Who's your guardian?"

"I'm Gemini, so it's a motorbike messenger guy called Hermie. Hermie for Hermes, for Mercury. He's Dr Cronus's grandson."

Mrs Hamilton shook her head. "Hermie? The gorgeous *Hermie?* No. It's not possible. He used to bring the post up on his bicycle when I was here. He was oh, about nineteen, maybe twenty, looked like a Greek god. We all had the biggest crushes on him, all of us vying for his attention and trying to get him to give us a ride on his bike. Sadly I never won. Ah but

167

he must be ancient by now. Well, older than me."

"No. No," said Ruth. "He still looks about twenty. I wonder if he's the same person?"

"I reckon he is," I said, "or the same being." I looked at Mrs Hamilton. "You must have seen him whizzing up and down on his motorbike."

She shook her head. "No. No I haven't. But then, so many people pass us by at Chiron House as if we're invisible in there. Then again, as you know, I haven't been there long. I used to live in my own house until… well, until it became clear I couldn't manage it anymore."

"We think Dr Cronus may be Saturn. I don't suppose he was here in your day." said Ruth.

Mrs Hamilton nodded. "Oh yes, Old Cronus we used to call him. He was here all right. I've just been in having a chat with him. He looked old then. I just thought he was one of those people who always looked ancient. And he still does. I didn't know that he was Hermie's grandfather though. Well I never!" She clapped her hands. "But this is too exciting! Another Zodiac Girl. No wonder so much has been going on! I didn't know what had hit me when it was my time. It changed my whole life, and I'll certainly never forget it." Then she laughed. "And they will *certainly* never forget me."

"Why? What happened?" asked Ruth.

Mrs Hamilton smiled mischievously. "I burnt down the science lab. Didn't mean to. Of course I didn't. It was Uri. He was my guardian. Uri for Uranus. He rules Aquarius. I was a very shy child. Timid as a mouse. He told me I had to experiment. I realized later that he meant in life – not in the chemistry lab!"

Ruth and I gasped.

"Yes," continued Mrs Hamilton. "Uranus brings the unexpected. It's symbolised by a bolt of lightening sometimes. Tee-hee. What I did was certainly unexpected. Mixed a few chemicals together in the spirit of discovery and trying to do what Uri had instructed me to, when kabang, blast and kerpow. No more science lab. Luckily no one was hurt but I was expelled and sent to school in Switzerland. Uri told me that I was to make a difference and I did! Not in the way I expected though. That's why later in life, I became a benefactor to the school. I wanted to make up for my... er... somewhat explosive time here."

Ruth and I both laughed.

"So, Gemma Whiting," continued Mrs Hamilton, "all I can say is, don't you worry. It took me a while but I made it right in the end. *Am* making it right. This school would have closed long ago without my help. Sometimes it's a mystery in life, but good can come from disaster. If I hadn't felt indebted to the school, I would never have felt the need to help keep it going."

"So you think I might get expelled, and maybe later, when I'm rich or famous, I'll come back and give them some dosh?"

Mrs Hamilton burst out laughing. "Oh no. Nothing like that. We all have our individual paths to tread. No. With you, I don't think it's going to take quite so long to find your calling."

She had a mischievous glint in her eye again. Oh dear, I thought. She blew up the science lab. What on earth does she think I'll end up doing?

Chapter Eighteen
Awards

It was the evening before the last day of term and everyone was ready for the performance of *Bugsy*. The school had been decorated for Christmas and a tall tree covered in red bows and baubles stood in the hall and the corridors were strewn with ivy, holly and tinsel. Some of the Year Eleven's had made decorations out of cinnamon sticks, cloves and orange peel and had hung them from ceilings so that everywhere smelt as well as looked festive.

The show was due to start at seven thirty but everyone, pupils, parents and guests alike, had been asked to be in their seats in the assembly hall for seven for a short prize-giving ceremony.

"Well, we made it to the end of term," I said to Ruth as we filed in and took the seats that Tasha had saved for us on the left-hand side of the hall.

"Yeah, phew!" she said. "And you were so sure that old Cronus was going to expel you. That time seems like ages ago now."

"I know. You know what was weird though? He never said anything more about it."

"Maybe Mrs Hamilton put in a good word for you," suggested Ruth.

"Maybe. But even if she did I can't believe Cronus would listen. You know what he's like. Maybe he thought he'd let me see the rest of term out and then it will be like, Happy Christmas, oh and by the way, you're expelled."

"No way. Surely he wouldn't be that mean?" said Ruth as she waved to my mum and dad who were seated half way back on the guest side of the hall. She'd become good friends with them since the beginning of term plus she was going to be spending Christmas holidays with us as her parents were still abroad and her alternative would have been staying at the school with Dr Cronus and other pupils who had parents out of the country. On the row behind Mum and Dad, Hermie was seated with Nessa and Joe. Hermie saw me and gave me the thumbs-up.

"Have you seen Sara preening herself?" asked Ruth as she glanced over the cast from the show who were seated in the front of the hall so that they could get backstage quickly when the prize giving was over. "She's probably hoping for one of the awards tonight but there are only three to be given out according to Mrs Blain so she'd be lucky if she got one."

I glanced over to where Ruth had been looking. It was the first time all the cast had been in full costume as even though there had been a dress rehearsal the week before, Mrs Woods had a superstition about not wearing costume until the night of the show and so wouldn't let anyone get into their outfits until tonight in case anything happened. They looked great, Sara in particular, and I couldn't help but feel a stab of envy. She had her hair slicked back into a bun at the back of her head and had pulled a kiss curl out over her forehead just like Jodie Foster had in the film. She was wearing full make up, a gorgeous grey silk slip of a dress and around her neck, she had a baby pink feather boa. She saw me looking at her, blew me a kiss and gave me a fake smile. I smiled back. I didn't care any more about her horrid treatment. I had real friends now and that was what mattered.

Dr Cronus got up onto the stage and the hall grew quiet in anticipation.

"I'd like to welcome everyone," said Dr Cronus as he looked out at the rows of people in front of him. "I'm so happy to see so many of you have turned out for our end of term show and so I won't keep you long. I'd just like to say that we're very lucky to have a most esteemed guest with us this evening. She's been a tremendous support to our school both in the past and in the present so I'd like you all to give a very warm welcome to the honourable Mrs Hamilton."

I almost got the giggles as Dr Cronus giving anyone a warm *anything* was a stretch of the imagination, as was the idea of him being happy to see everyone there. He looked his usual glum self as he stood there on the stage.

A moment later, Fleur was seen helping Mrs Hamilton up the stairs to join the headmaster.

She stood at the podium and looked around her. "Good evening," she said. "As an old pupil of the school, I can't tell you what a great pleasure it is to be back here. It always brings back many happy memories and many... many er, shall I say, not so happy ones. School days can be a rollercoaster for all of us. Good times, bad times. But I'm not here to bore you with my reminiscences. I'm not here to talk about the past. I'm here to talk about the future. As you know there have been various projects happening around the school to raise funds. The school play..."

At this point, I saw Sara sit up a little straighter as though she was waiting for an acknowledgement. She also reached up to her neck, gave it a good scratch and a bit of her hair came out of its clip at the back.

Ruth must have noticed too because she nudged me. "Looks like Sara's feather boa might have fleas," she giggled. "She's been scratching herself since she sat down."

"... I look forward to seeing it immensely in a moment so I won't keep you too long," Mrs Hamilton continued. "And of course there's the Outreach programme."

Ruth nudged me while Sara turned and sneered.

"Yes. The Outreach programme which I believe got off to a... how can I put this? A... *hair-raising* start but there are plans to keep it developing and I do hope that more of you will be inspired to take part. Now. To the awards. It's always been the tradition at Avebury to give praise where it's due, encouragement where it's deserved and admonishment where it's needed. I can't say how pleased I am to be here in person this year to give these awards out myself. It's one of the perks of being one of the school's benefactors. So let's get started. The first award goes to the pupil who has done the best academically so far and that goes to Sophie Johnson in Year Eleven. Well done and come forward Sophie."

A dark-haired girl I didn't know made her way forward to the stage and was given a huge box of chocolates and a mini iPod.

"Well done," said Mrs Hamilton as she shook Sophie's hand. "Now for heaven's sake, lighten up and get a life, girl. Chill a bit. A happy life means a balance between hard work *and* pleasure."

Everyone looked at each other in amazement,

especially the parents. This wasn't like prize giving in my old school.

"Next," said Mrs Hamilton. "An award for the most lazy girl in school. Maisie Pickford come forward."

Maisie Pickford went bright red but made her way up onto the stage where she was given an arm-load of study books.

"And you, young lady. You have a brain," said Mrs Hamilton. "Now use it."

A few girls in Year Ten started laughing.

"Right, who's next?" asked Mrs Hamilton. "Oh yes. The next award is for the pupil who has shown the most promise this term."

At the front, Sara smoothed back her hair and had another scratch.

"This is the one I reckon Sara's after," whispered Ruth.

"And the winner is... Gemma Whiting," called Mrs Hamilton.

"Oh my god!" I exclaimed. "That's me."

Ruth beamed at me, pushed me off my chair and towards the stage where moments later, I climbed up and stood next to a smiling Mrs Hamilton.

"I've chosen Gemma for this award," she said, "because she's only been here a term and despite a difficult start, she's made excellent progress, and no thanks to many of you in this room according to what

I've heard from Mrs Blain and some of the other teachers. It's hard changing schools after Year Seven when you're beginning together and all in the same boat. In future, I'm going to ask all of you to be more sensitive to the people around you who are new or don't know the ropes as well as you do and that goes for the parents and friends here tonight too, whatever the situation you're in. Don't be selfish. Give out the hand of friendship or else... you'll have me to answer to and I may be old but I can be tough!"

A cheer came from the right and I looked over to see that it had come from Hermie who was grinning up at Mrs Hamilton.

She beamed back at him. "As you know, a lot of the money raised this year will go to building the new science lab. But I thought of something else I'd like to see developed here. I'm going to have a new wing built for the Outreach programme where anyone who wants can go on a Friday afternoon and train in various skills. I'm going to invite all the leading experts in their fields to come and talk to you. You can train to do beauty so that you can take those skills with you into hospitals and homes... *and*," she gave me a huge smile at this point, "I shall invite some of the experts from the animal-therapy programmes so that you can learn about taking animals in."

At the mention of the word animals, a soft groan

came from the front row. I looked down and got the feeling that it was Sara who had made the noise. She was certainly looking unhappy.

"Gemma was quite right in her idea that animals can give tremendous comfort to the old, the infirm, the lonely," Mrs Hamilton continued. "In fact, I've already hired an expert in that field and he's going to be here at the start of next term. All this was inspired by the girl standing here in front of you. She wanted to make a difference and I'd like you all to learn from her. And because of that, I'm going to call the scheme the Gemma Whiting project."

I felt myself going bright red but Mrs Hamilton hadn't finished.

"Now I know I'm an old lady and you probably all think I'm a bit barmy but I can tell you one thing. There's nothing more miserable in this life than being lonely and feeling left out. People feel it in schools. People feel it in work. People feel it when they're old. Be aware and do what you can. Take a little time out from thinking about yourself all the time. There's a lot of suffering in the world and it's not all in far off places. Be aware of what's happening around you. On your doorstep. In your home, your neighbourhood, your school."

Everyone in the hall looked at each other, back at the stage and then a cheer went up, this time from some Year Elevens on the back rows. Soon the rest of the hall joined in with them. Rose, Grace, Imogen, Ruth and Tasha were all grinning like idiots and giving me the thumbs-up. I could hardly believe what was happening.

"Would you like to say something, Gemma?" asked Mrs Hamilton.

I shook my head but she nudged me towards the podium.

I took a deep breath and looked out on the sea of faces in front of me.

"I… I didn't want to come here at first," I said. "And it's true, I found my first few weeks hard going, that first month in fact but… but, well, if my time here has shown me anything, it's that, as Mrs Hamilton said, life *is* a rollercoaster. Up and down we go. New challenges, new obstacles. I've learnt never to give up because you never know what the future holds and what each new day will bring. Um. That's all, I think."

A cheer rose again from the back of the hall and I looked out to see rows of smiling faces. Apart from Sara's that is. She looked very strange. Like someone had blown her up with a bicycle pump. Her lips were swollen, her eyes were bulging out of their sockets and her face was covered in nasty red blotches and sweat, her hair had come out of its immaculate style and was sticking all over her face like wet straw. And she was clawing at her face as if it was on fire.

"Oh Lord. Oh dear. Oh heck," cried Mrs Woods getting to her feet when she saw Sara fall to her knees and start groaning. "Quick someone, get the matron! Get the doctor!"

It seemed like everything went into fast gear. The matron and the doctor were called and rushed to the front. Someone brought a bowl of water and began splashing Sara's face. I got down from the stage and went back to join Ruth. An ambulance was called for. Guests were ushered off into the dining area for pre-show drinks and Mrs Woods started dancing about like she had ants in her pants trying to get the rest of the cast backstage.

A stretcher was brought from the sick room and four Year Elevens picked Sara up and laid her on it. They carried her down the aisle with the doctor and matron following behind. Just as they reached where Ruth, Tasha and I were sitting, Sara peered out at me through bulgy toad-like eyes. She looked awful. Nothing like the pretty girl she was. She looked like a monster. She raised a swollen finger and pointed. "All your fault," she moaned as she was carried off.

"*Me*? What did I do?" I asked the others.

"Nothing," said Tasha stepping forward and linking my arm. "Take no notice. I think I know *exactly* what's happened. She's allergic to animals. That boa around her neck was the real thing. Genuine ostrich feathers."

"Allergic to animals?" Ruth repeated. "Ohmigod! Bertie!"

"Bertie?" I asked. "What's he got to do with it?"

"Remember that day your dad brought him and I found him?"

"Yeah. So?"

"Do you remember *where* I found him?"

"Er... oh! Yes. In the drama room!"

"In the *costume* department to be precise and now that I remember, he was curled up very comfortably on a pale pink boa."

"And come to think of it, Boris the cat likes to sneak in there for a sleep too. I've seen him a few times. It's next to the boiler room so it's cosy. Feathers, dog *and* cat hair! No wonder she had an allergic reaction."

"But will she be all right?" I asked. "She looked terrible."

Tasha nodded. "Not in time for the show but she'll be fine as soon as they've given her an anti-allergy injection. Same thing happened last summer when she came to stay with my family and our cat slept on her pillow one afternoon when we'd gone out. She blew up like a balloon when she got into bed later that night."

Ruth started giggling.

"What's so funny?" I asked.

"She said it was your fault and well... you *are* the Lady of the Beasts," she said then put on a spooky voice. "Beeeeewaaaaare the Lady of the Beasts. Her power must never be unleeeeeeeshed or eeeeeelse she will set her dog onto you."

Tasha started laughing too. "She did look awful, didn't she?" she asked. "And I know I shouldn't laugh but she'll be okay, really she will... but in the meantime, she's turned from goddess to geek. Serves her right. I hope someone got a photo of her."

At that moment, Mrs Woods came flying into the hall and looked around frantically.

"Gemma, Gemma," she called.

I raced over.

"You're on. Five minutes. Oh Lord. Oh dear. Oh heck. The show must go on."

"Me? On? And do what?"

"Tallulah of course," said Mrs Woods as she beckoned me into the backstage area. "You're the only one who knows the part except for Sara!"

Behind her, I saw Hermie leaning against a pillar. He looked over at me and winked.

And so I got to play out my fantasy. All those days memorising Tallulah's words and driving Mum and Dad mad finally paid off as I took centre stage. The show was a terrific success. I gave it my all and had the most brilliant time ever and afterwards, everyone said it was one of the best shows that the school had ever put on. As I got changed back into my normal clothes, Mrs Woods took me aside and said that I had "saved the day".

After the show was over, guests began to drift out towards the car park and I walked Mrs Hamilton out to the front to say thank you and goodbye.

"Where's your car?" I asked as I looked around the courtyard for her Rolls Royce.

"Oh I sent it on," she said as a familiar figure roared up the driveway on his bike.

A few seconds later, Hermie drew up besides us.

He winked at me. "Had a good evening?" he asked with a grin.

"The best," I smiled back.

Hermie then pulled a helmet out of his carrier box on the back of his bike. I thought he was going to hand it to me and ask me to go for a ride but he handed it to Mrs Hamilton.

"Your carriage awaits, Ma'am," he said.

She blushed and for a moment looked like a coy teenager. She put on the helmet and hoisted herself up on the back of his bike with surprising agility then she put her arms around Hermie's waist.

"Hang on in there, Zodiac Girl," she smiled at me.

"You too, ZG," I smiled back.

"And I'll be watching out for you," said Hermie as he revved up his engine. "Just don't forget, the magic's all around you Gemma, inside and out. Make the most of it. It's your choice what you do with it. But for now, it's over and out."

"Yes sir," I said with a salute.

And with that, they roared off down the drive and out of sight.

The Gemini Files
Characteristics, Facts and Fun.

May 22 - June 21

Whether it's nattering on their mobile, gossiping with their friends or firing off emails, Geminis are great communicators and they love to talk, talk, talk! Persuasion is their middle name and they often charm people to get their way. They are multi-faceted, strong-willed and independent.

Geminis push themselves to the max with their sense of adventure and fun, but as a result can end up biting off more than they can chew. This can lead to confusion – but that's not surprising as their star symbol is the twins – showing a dual personality.

Element:	Air
Colour:	Yellow, silver
Birthstone:	Emerald/Agate
Animal:	Magpie
Lucky day:	Wednesday
Planet:	ruled by Mercury

Gemini best friends are likely to be:
Aries
Gemini
Sagittarius
Aquarius

Gemini enemies are likely to be:
Scorpio
Taurus

A Gemini's idea of heaven would be:
hosting their own prime time talk-show.

A Gemini would go mad if:
they were grounded without their phone
and computer.

Famous Geminis:
Naomi Campbell
Johnny Depp
Angelina Jolie
Nicole Kidman
Kylie Minogue

Here's the first chapter of another brilliant **Zodiac Girls** story, **Recipe for Rebellion**.

Chapter One

Bat Poo

"Danu Harvey Jones. Can you read us the poem you've written about family?" asked Mr Beecham peering over his glasses at the front of the classroom. "And sit up straight, girl."

"It's Dee, not Danu," I said.

"I think not, Miss Harvey Jones. We call ourselves by our proper names at this school. We don't use nicknames and your given name is Danu. Now, stand up and read us your poem."

I stood up and took a deep breath.

"My aunt is full of bat poo,
My brother is a twit,
My parents have deserted me,
I don't know where I fit."

A few girls at the back of class tittered as Mr Beecham's mouth shrunk to look like a cat's bottom.

"That's enough Danu," he said. "Sit down. I don't

think we need to hear any more of that. See me after class."

I sat down. I'd probably get detention again. I didn't care. At least there would be a few people around in there and it would be better than going back to the empty flat. Again.

Joele Morrison was next up reading her poem. I rolled my eyes. It was about a cute kitten playing on the grass and her ickle lickle baby brother rolling into a flower bed. Blah. Vomitous and a half. My poem had at least told the truth about my situation and what else was I supposed to write? About kittens and babies? Yeah right. A kitten would die of malnutrition where I was living now and as for an ickle lickle brother, there was just no space, in fact, there was only just enough space for me.

For the rest of the lesson as my fellow schoolmates droned on with their pathetic poems, I gazed out of the window and thought about my old life. What were my old friends doing at this moment as I sat here having to endure Death by Bad Poetry? I hated my life. I hated my new school. I hated everyone in it. My world was rotten. It wasn't always like this. I didn't always live in the hellhole that I do now. No. Once I had a life. A life I was very happy with thank you very much. I lived in a village down on the south coast with my dad who's an archaeologist.

He's famous is some circles. My mum died when I was three so my dad had a lady from the village come in and housekeep for us. Mrs Wilkins. She was lovely. Kind and jolly and the most brilliant cook. There was always the smell of something wonderful baking in the oven when I got home. I attended the local school and in fact I was able to walk there from our old house. It took ten minutes, through the back field, five minutes along the coast road and there I was. I had loads of mates. Bernie, Fran, Annie and Jane. I had a dog, Snowy (he was jet black). I had a cat, Blackie (he was pure white) and I used to be able to ride our neighbour's horse. They let me name him so I called him Spot (he was a chestnut). There were birds and squirrels in our garden. I had a huge bedroom with a bay window looking out over rolling fields and woods. I was happy.

One day, Dad was waiting for me when I came home from school. I could tell the moment I set eyes on him that something was wrong. At first I thought someone had died or something had happened to Snowy or Blackie. But no. Nothing like that. Dad had been offered a year's contract working on some ancient site in South America digging up old bones and stuff. Chance of a lifetime. The one he'd been waiting for. Etc etc. Blah de blah de blah. And that was the end of life as I knew it.

Why couldn't he go and leave me with Mrs Wilkins as usually happened when there was a dig? I asked. But he wouldn't hear of it. Other digs had been for a weekend, a fortnight at the longest. This was the big one and would take him away for a whole year. I begged to be able to stay at the house but he'd already arranged for it to be rented out for the year. Nothing I could say or do could persuade him to let me stay. I tried to fix it so I could live with one of my mates but no-one had room. I'd be "just fine," said Dad. He'd arranged for me to attend a boarding school near where his sister lived. He'd be back to see me in the holidays and my aunt would keep an eye on me in the meantime. I was a grown up girl. I'd soon adjust. That was the time I realised that he cared more about a load of old dead bones than he did about me, his living daughter.

"Danu, *Danu,*" said a stern voice in my ear. It was old Beecham again. What did he want now?

"Yes, sir."

"Have you been listening to anything that is going on in this lesson?"

"Yes, sir. Kittens. Ickle babies."

Mr Beecham sighed then went back to the front of the room. "Class dismissed," he said.

I got up to go with the others.

"Not you, Harvey Jones. I want a word."

I slumped back down into my chair. I was very popular with the teachers at this school. They were always keeping me back for "a word".

Mr Beecham waited as the rest of the class filed out. A few of the girls turned and stared at me then whispered to each other. I stuck my tongue out at them.

When the others had gone, Mr Beecham came and sat at the desk opposite and looked at me with concern.

"So Danu. How are you settling in?"

I shrugged. "Okay."

He sighed again. "And how's life at home?"

"Not at home..."

"Ah yes, I meant your home now. I believe you're living with your aunt?"

I shrugged again. "Yeah."

"And are things all right there?"

"Yeah." I wasn't going to tell him the truth. There was no point. Nobody could do anything to get me out of there.

Mr Beecham coughed. "Well Danu... I'm afraid we're going to have to do something, aren't we? About your attitude."

I shifted my feet and looked out of the window.

"Have you got any suggestions?" Mr Beecham persisted. "And please look at me when I'm talking to you."

I turned back to him. "Whatever."

"Whatever is not an answer. I have your records from your past school, Danu, so you don't fool me. You were a straight-A pupil and now your highest mark is D. What are you going to do about it?"

"Work harder," I muttered. I had no intention of working harder. My plan was to get expelled and then with a bit of luck, I could go back to my old school. Even if it meant living in the dog kennel with Snowy, I wouldn't mind.

Mr Beecham stood up. "I hope so Danu. I hope so. We're here to help you know, not hinder, so I'd appreciate a bit of an effort on your part. And… I also need to talk to you about… well about your hair…"

"What about it?" I asked. It had taken me months to get it into decent dreadlocks. As my hair is fine and reddish blonde, it had taken weeks and weeks of twirling and twirling before the coils stayed but at last they were starting to look the business. I'd even wound some green and pink wool through some of them. My dreadlocks were part of my plan. I had to look the part of a rebel as well as act it.

"Well… don't you ever comb it?"

"No way."

"But that can't be hygienic."

I shrugged. "Is there a rule that says I can't wear my hair like this?"

"Not exactly."

"So what's the problem?"

"It makes you look, well, how can I put this... rather unkempt."

"Do you tell other girls how to wear their hair?"

"No. I don't make a habit of it."

"Right then. Can I go now?"

Mr Beecham sighed. "I suppose so."

I made my way out of the school and through the playground to the bus stop. Girls were still hanging about, chatting, having a laugh. I kept my head down. I wished I had a mate here. I wished I had someone's house I could go to and hang out in, gossiping about the day, about fellow pupils. But no, the only place I had to go back to was the prison of a flat where I lived with my aunt, the warden.

She lives in a small flat on the fifteenth floor of a tall block in a new development area. No grass, no trees, no animals and no outside access except for a tiny balcony with one dead pot plant on it. Aunt Esme earns good dosh at her job but she chooses to live in this no man's land because it's an easy commute to her work. Okay for her as she's never home. I felt like I was suffocating there. There's nothing to do. Nowhere to go as it's not safe after dark because of its proximity to a rough estate. I was going to end up like that poor geranium on the balcony. Dead.

I caught the bus and sat looking out at the gloomy winter's night. The clocks had gone back last week so it was dark early. On the streets, people were huddled into their coats rushing to get home out of the cold. I got off in the square where Aunt Esme lives and sloped over to her block. Up the steps, into the door, into the lift that smelt damp, of boiled cabbage, and up to her floor. It was like being in some sci fi film about the future where all traces of natural life had been destroyed and all that was left was concrete.

I let myself into the flat, turned on the lights and went into the sitting room to turn on the TV. I always did that the minute I got back as the sounds of people on the telly made me feel as if I wasn't totally alone. I slumped down to watch. No point in going to the fridge. Aunt Esme didn't buy proper food, only posh assorted lettuce in polythene bags. And sometimes there was a lemon in there for her gin and tonic drink. She never cooked at home as she ate out most evenings with her job or grabbed something at the office where she usually worked late.

At six o'clock precisely there was a knock at the door. It was Rosa bringing my supper. She works as Aunt Esme's cleaner and when I moved in, she was hired to bring me my supper every evening as well.

She's Polish, about twenty, and hardly speaks any English.

She came into the hall and pointed towards the kitchen.

"Shall put in microwiv?" she asked.

"No, I'll take it," I replied. "Thank you."

She handed me the dish then left.

She wasn't a bad cook actually, although her repertoire was somewhat limited. Some sort of goulashy thing with carrots and beans every night. *Still better than soggy lettuce*, I thought as I heated it up and took it back to eat while I watched TV.

I'd heated it up too much and the first forkful burnt the inside of my mouth. I felt tears prick the back of my eyes.

"Bat poo," I said to the empty room.

I had never felt so alone in all of my life.